Rose Cottage
— BOOK CLUB —

Every Trick in the Book

Tara Johnson

Annie's®
AnniesFiction.com

Books in the Rose Cottage Book Club series

Library of Congress-in-Publication Data
Every Trick in the Book / by Tara Johnson
p. cm.
I. Title
                    2022935185

AnniesFiction.com
(800) 282-6643
Rose Cottage Book Club™
Series Creator: Shari Lohner
Series Editor: Kristen Susienka
Cover Illustrator: Jo Tronc

10 11 12 13 14 | Printed in South Korea | 9 8 7 6 5 4 3 2 1

Luke

"There." Luke Harris stepped back and admired his handiwork. His favorite painting of Winston Churchill finally had a place on his law office wall. Now he could enjoy it as often as he liked while he worked.

The space around him had come a long way in the few weeks since he'd signed the lease. The walls, once a nearly blinding white, now sported a calming blue-gray hue more appropriate for business dealings with a range of clients. An executive desk faced the door, ready to welcome all who entered, and two oversize plants stretched their fronds behind it. Tucked in the corner was a file cabinet and a smaller table where a coffeepot and an assortment of syrups, creamers, and sugar waited. Twin paneled windows overlooked the main street. If Luke stepped outside, he knew he'd see the pink glow of Rose Cottage Books next door.

Walking down a small hallway, he placed the hammer he'd used in the lone supply closet and paused. His late wife, Jeanine, had possessed an expert eye for decorating—she would have loved helping him here. Even though four years had passed since her death, the hollow ache in his chest still rose up every now and then. She'd had such a knack for color and aesthetic, and for finding joy in little projects—like hanging up artwork. Could she see how far he'd come?

He hoped she could. Her passing had uprooted his life in so many ways, but he knew she and their little one were always watching over him. He was sure they had had a hand in bringing him here. Moving to Nantucket had given him a new sense of direction and new dreams to pursue. He was finally beginning to feel like himself again.

Thank you.

He returned to his office and had just dropped into the soft leather chair behind his desk when the front door opened, letting in the briny scent of the ocean. A middle-aged woman with dark, curly hair and striking blue eyes bustled into the room.

"Mr. Harris?"

Luke rose from his chair and offered her a hand. "Hello, ma'am. How can I help you?"

Without shaking his outstretched hand, the woman took the chair opposite him. "My name is Stella Jones. I'd like to offer you some business."

He started at that. Not many clients were so direct. "Of course. What can I do for you, Mrs. Jones? And would you like a cup of coffee while we talk?"

"Yes, thank you. Two sugars, one cream." She straightened as Luke went to get her a cup and refill his own, which had been cooling on his desk. "I would like to hire you as my attorney. I intend to sue my son-in-law for defamation of character."

Luke handed her a mug, then resumed his seat. Had he heard the woman correctly? *Sue her son-in-law?* "Pardon me, Mrs. Jones, but your request is surprising. Can you explain?"

She lifted her chin. "It's quite simple, Mr. Harris. My son-in-law has been dragging me through the mud, and I want it stopped immediately."

"What has he done?"

Stella sighed. "Antonio is a comic. He thinks he's a good one, and many agree, but I'm not so sure." Her nose wrinkled as if smelling something noxious. "I told my daughter, Missy, he was no good from the very beginning. What kind of a career is being a comedian, anyway?

You can't support a family on an income like that, surely."

"Oh, I don't know. Some do pretty we—"

"But did Missy listen to me? No." She grimaced and took a sip of coffee. "My daughter married a man who now spends his days writing jokes about *me* and then blabbing them to every comedy club in the area. He's even on the Internet. Go ahead. Take a look."

She fixed him with a stare, and after a few moments, Luke realized she actually wanted him to do as she said. He turned to his computer and brought up a search engine. "What is your son-in-law's name?"

Stella pinched the bridge of her nose as she spoke. "Antonio Poppalardo."

Luke typed in the name and pulled up a video of a young, dark-haired comic holding a microphone. He pressed Play, and the man's deep voice drifted through the speakers.

"So my mother-in-law comes up to me one day and says, 'I know you'll dance on my grave when I'm dead.' I told her, 'No way. You know how much I hate waiting in lines.'"

Luke winced as the audience howled, his gaze flickering to the woman before him. Her frown deepened as her son-in-law continued.

"My mother-in-law is banned internationally from playing poker. I mean, I don't blame the casinos. She always keeps the chips on her shoulder."

More laughter. Luke sighed.

"Some people call their in-laws their outlaws. A funny play on words. But I don't like that phrase. There's a big difference between the two. Outlaws are wanted."

Applause filtered through the speakers while Stella waved her hand as if shooing a pesky fly. Her cheeks glowed crimson. "I'm sure you get the idea, Mr. Harris." Luke clicked off the video as the woman went on. "Antonio's whole act is nothing but an attack to degrade and humiliate me. What do you think? Can we start the paperwork to begin a lawsuit?"

Luke leaned forward, resting his elbows on the desk. "Mrs. Jones, may I make a suggestion?"

"Please."

Luke carefully considered his words before he continued. "Lawsuits of this nature are very expensive and risky. Judges tend to rule in favor of the defendants, claiming First Amendment rights. I have an idea we might try instead."

"What's that?"

"I can mediate the conflict between you and Antonio. I'm a licensed mediator, and I think we could see this issue resolved in a satisfactory manner."

Stella stared into her coffee cup, seeming to mull over the idea. "I suppose it's worth a try."

"I promise I'll do all I can." Luke pushed a pad of paper and a pen across the desk. "Please write down his name and contact information. I'd like to try to set up the mediation for some time next week, provided it works with both of your schedules. We'll see what he has to say."

Stella shifted and set her coffee cup on the corner of the desk. "I don't have his number. I just bought a new phone and haven't transferred any of my contacts."

"Do you know of another way I can reach him?"

"Here." She grabbed the paper and scribbled something onto it.

Turning it around, Luke read the words aloud. "The Bad Punchline."

"It's a comedy club he frequents here in Nantucket. Performs there several times a week. His next show is Sunday night. You could meet him there."

She wants me to hunt down her son-in-law at a comedy club? An unusual request. "I'll see what I can do."

When they'd finished discussing the particulars of mediation and fees involved for the service, Stella rose, clutching her purse.

"Thank you, Mr. Harris. The coffee was lovely too."

She swept out and Luke reached for his mug of coffee. Somehow, he had the nagging suspicion this mediation wouldn't be an easy task. *What makes a comic tick, anyway? And why is he so intent on aggravating his mother-in-law?*

After cleaning up the coffee mugs, Luke headed next door to Rose Cottage Books. Law was his forte, but comedy—not so much. He hoped there was something in a book he could learn to even the playing field.

Luke ran his finger over the book he'd taken off the shelf. *Comedy Writing 101. Probably a good place to start learning the art of humor.* He flipped to the contents page and read the names of the chapters out loud to himself. "'Observe the World Around You,' 'Use Your Own Life,' 'The Rule of Threes,' 'How Not to Be a Hack.' Very interesting."

Tucking the book under his arm, Luke was starting toward the register when a yip at his feet caught his attention. Hash Brown, the unofficial ambassador of Rose Cottage Books, stared up at him, his stubby tail wagging.

Luke chuckled to the French bulldog. "Well, hello there, Hash Brown. How are you today?"

The dog barked happily while Luke reached down to scratch his long, pointed ears.

Bookshop owner Meagan Poe rounded the corner, a smile on her face and her chocolate-brown eyes twinkling. Luke enjoyed seeing his friend whenever he stopped in, grateful for her business on the island. She'd told him that she had been a middle school librarian before opening Rose Cottage Books about a year ago. He could see why kids would have loved her as a librarian, but he was glad she had made the career change.

"I wondered what made Hash Brown disappear so fast. Your buddy missed you, I see. Every time you pass by the window with more office supplies, he tries to get me to take him outside."

Luke grinned. "It's good to have a loyal friend. And you know he's welcome to visit if he likes. You both are."

"I'll keep that in mind. How's the office coming along?"

"Fine. I've been decorating lots lately. It's looking more like a workplace by the minute."

Meagan smiled. "Wonderful. So, what brings you in today? *Comedy Writing 101*?" Her lips quirked as she glimpsed the book in his hand. "Got tired of our history selection?"

Luke chuckled. "Hardly. It's research for a client."

Her expression said she wanted to ask more, but she didn't press him. Instead, she waved him toward the register. "If you're ready, I'll ring up your book."

"That would be great. Thanks, Meagan."

While waiting to pay, he studied the sign advertising the book club at the end of the counter. "How's your book club going?"

"It's great. We have a wonderful time together. You're welcome to join us whenever you'd like. Our next meeting is today, in fact. Five thirty this evening."

He handed her his credit card. "I think I can swing by. Does it matter if I haven't read the book?"

"Not at all. We start by summarizing what everyone's read so far. As long as you don't mind spoilers, there's no problem."

"That's fine with me."

"Good. The book this month is *When Fireflies Dance*. It's a newer historical romance."

Luke's lips curved into a grin. "Believe it or not, I have read that one."

Meagan straightened her glasses. "Have you? That's great. You'll fit right in."

"I'll do my best." With that, he turned to leave. "See you later. You too, Hash Brown."

The dog followed him as far as the front door, then gazed after him with his large, sad brown eyes as Luke headed to the next building over.

Luke took no more than a few steps into his office before he stopped. He wasn't alone. A well-dressed woman sat in the chair Stella Jones had previously occupied. She wore a long skirt, a turquoise blouse, and gold earrings that glinted in the light beneath her silver hair. He noticed that more jewels decorated her fingers and draped around her neck. *She makes a statement.*

Luke hurried to his desk and set the book inside a top drawer. "Good morning. Forgive me for keeping you. I wasn't expecting anyone."

"Please. No apologies necessary. I've enjoyed studying your office unobserved. You can tell a lot about a man by how he decorates his place of business." The woman fixed him with a hard stare. "You love history. Or maybe strong leaders."

Luke smiled, taking in the woman's aged but pleasant face. Wrinkles covered her cheeks and forehead, and the hands she'd folded in front of her bent slightly with age. "Both," he said. "You are a very astute woman, Miss—?"

"Honey Northcutt, Mr. Harris. I can tell you're new to Nantucket because anyone who's been here very long knew my late husband, George." She fluffed her silver hair. "I also found out you're new because my daughter, Alexis, told me. She read about you in the *Dolphin Gazette*. I understand they did a small feature on your law office opening up."

"Yes, they did." With all the excitement of setting up his office, he'd almost forgotten about that.

"Alexis enjoyed it very much. I did too, which is why I'm here now."

"I see. I appreciate you thinking of me." Luke rose and gestured to the coffee maker. "Care for a cup of coffee, Mrs. Northcutt?"

"Yes, that is very kind of you."

"Sugar or cream?"

"Black, please." She shook her head. "I can't abide anything but plain old coffee in my coffee. Any extra flavor ruins the taste."

"I can understand that." After placing a warm cup in the woman's hand, Luke eased into his chair. "Now, how can I help you?"

She took a sip and shifted. "I would like you to adjust my will. For years I've had my daughter, Alexis, and son, Hunter, written out of my estate. But I want you to help me change that."

"Yes, I can do that for you." One of Luke's specialties was estate management. Back on the mainland, he'd had a fair number of older clients—and some younger ones—who wanted to prepare for the future. He could help this woman too.

Mrs. Northcutt twirled a ring on her finger as she spoke. "I've kept my children out of my will for personal reasons. You know how it is. Some children grow up to be spoiled adults. And unfortunately, mine are two prime examples. Or, I should say, they were. For years Alexis flitted from job to job and relationship to relationship, trying to maintain the affluent lifestyle George and I gave her." Pain flashed through the woman's eyes. "Hunter ended up in prison. Partying with the wrong people taught him hard lessons."

"I'm sorry."

She straightened and took another sip of coffee. "Don't be. However, of late, I have seen positive changes in both of them. Their hearts are softening. Hunter's just been released too. Perhaps it's maturity. Perhaps it's my prayers."

Luke smiled gently. "Prayer certainly changes things."

Honey placed her mug on the desk. "Whatever the cause, I'm ready to change my will—not only for them, but for other reasons." She reached into her purse and removed a manila folder, which she handed to Luke. "Here. This is my current will. The paper on top is how I would like it redistributed. Can I count on you, Mr. Harris?"

Luke studied the contents inside the folder, then set it on his desk. "Yes. In fact, my schedule is pretty open for a Tuesday. I should have this done in a few hours. I will call when I'm finished and you can stop by at your convenience to sign the papers."

"That will do fine. Thank you. I'll waste no more of your time now." The older woman rose, took a business card from Luke's desk, and tucked it into her purse. "If I have any questions, I'll call. But I promise not to be one of those customers who calls you in the middle of the night."

Luke chuckled, rising to walk her to the exit. "I appreciate that."

The older woman patted his arm. "I think you and I are going to get along fine."

"I completely agree."

Luke closed the door behind her and gazed through his office windows at the bustling street outside. He couldn't help but smile at the progress of the day and the thrill of contentment coursing through him.

Two new clients before noon. Yes, it's good to be in business again.

2

Meagan

"You're not thinking of buying another fish, are you, Nan?" Meagan asked as she carried a plate of her prized lemon cake from the office to the seating area where the book club would soon gather. Setting it on a table in the center of the circle of chairs, she smiled to her grandmother. Nell Poe sat in a blue-gray chair embroidered with white seashells. Her body hunched forward slightly, letting Meagan know how focused she was on the last pages of the book club novel. So focused, in fact, that she seemed to have missed Meagan's question.

"Nan?" Meagan tried again.

Her grandmother startled, peering over the top of the book. "Oh, the book is wonderful, Meagan. Excellent choice."

Meagan shook her head with a smile. "I'm glad you enjoy it." She peered down at the stack of books near the woman's feet. *Exotic Fish of the World* caught her attention once more. "I was asking if you're thinking of getting more fish."

Nell set the book club book aside and followed Meagan's gaze. "Oh. Yes, dear. That's for research. Nemo, Skittles, and Long John Silver get lonely, so I thought it was time I bought them some friends."

Meagan pictured the fish tank inside her grandmother's Federal-style home. It had once teemed with aquatic life, but it had slowly become less populated over the last few months. More fish would certainly brighten up the space. "Fair enough."

She scanned the book club area and grinned, delighting in the assortment of sweet and savory selections she'd arranged on the table. *Lots of choices for everyone today.* To Nell, she said, "I have a good feeling about the book club meeting tonight."

Nell chuckled. "Remind me why you decided to have it on a Tuesday rather than the customary Saturday?"

"Well, I was hoping to test out a different day to see if it attracts more members," Meagan explained. "Tuesday afternoons are busier than most Saturday afternoons because we're open until eight tonight, while we close at four on Saturdays. If more visitors see the book club meeting, maybe they'll join us and help spread the word."

Nell nodded. "By the way," she said, "I stopped in at Sea Breeze Yarns earlier. Dwayne Wright was there picking up some yarn for his wife. He told me a joke to pass along to you."

Meagan smirked. Dwayne, one of Nantucket's oldest residents, was known for his bad jokes. "Okay. Let's hear it."

"He said you should never date a fisherman. All he'd do is string you along."

Meagan groaned. "That's terrible. He should keep his dating advice to himself." She made a final tweak to the circle of chairs that would welcome book club members. "There. I think we're all set."

Nell looked back to her book. "Is it almost five thirty, dear?"

"Yes. Less than an hour to go."

"Good. Plenty of time to finish." Nell went back to reading.

Meagan smiled and left her grandmother to it, then headed to the front of the store. She called to Hash Brown, who scampered over as fast as his little legs could carry him, his tongue lolling in happiness. "Let's go see what Hattie's up to."

The dog panted in agreement.

They found the woman helping a customer at the register. "Hi, Hattie."

"Oh, hello, Meagan," Hattie answered as she tore the customer's receipt from the machine and handed it to him. "Done setting up for book club?"

"Yes. It's always more work than I think, but so worth it."

Hattie smiled. "Expecting any new members today?"

"Luke will be there, and maybe some others."

Hattie's smile grew. "Luke Harris, our new neighborhood attorney?"

"Yes. It's his first time joining, so I hope he likes it. If nothing else, it'll be nice to have a man's perspective for a change. And who knows? Maybe his participation will encourage other men to give it a try."

"I see."

Meagan straightened. Hattie Peabody, part-time employee and full-time friend, clearly had more to say. "What?"

Hattie shrugged. "I heard Luke is single. He's also quite handsome, and you are an attractive woman—"

"Hattie." Meagan rolled her eyes. "He's only coming to a book club meeting. Nothing more."

"I know. I know." The woman's expression softened, her gaze growing wistful. "I want you to be happy."

"Thank you. I appreciate it, but I'm perfectly happy as I am." Thoughts of her last boyfriend, Carl Issacs, and his deception a year and a half ago with his coworker Alicia Hearst resurfaced, but she quickly flicked them away. She had no space in her life for that kind of negativity. The relationship had ended, and she was a better woman for it. "I'm over Carl, truly, but I'm not ready to jump into dating yet. I'm happy to take my time."

"Not every man is like him, you know."

"True. But I'll know when the time is right for me to try again."

Hash Brown barked, protesting the lack of attention being paid to him.

Hattie crouched to pet the dog. "Good news, Hash Brown. You're still her main man. Help her pick someone nice, okay?"

Hash Brown yipped as if he accepted his mission gladly.

The shop door opened, causing the trio to look up as Piper Watts walked in, her arms loaded with shopping bags. Hash Brown, who took his duty as shop greeter seriously, was quick to dance around her ankles. Sunglasses sat perched atop the woman's curly, wind-blown brown hair as she heaved a sigh.

Meagan grinned. "Were you on a shopping spree?"

Her friend grimaced. "I wish. Believe it or not, all of this is research for new beauty articles Cooper wants over the next few weeks. He had me shop for the items this time rather than send things to me—a secret-shopper experience I hope not to relive anytime soon." She dropped the bags near the door, nearly tripping over the pile and Hash Brown in the process. "Most of the stores passed inspection."

Meagan smiled, knowing well that her friend enjoyed any hint of investigative journalism she could get nowadays despite her dramatic claims.

Hattie laughed. "I can't wait to read all about them."

"Jim will love seeing all these beauty products cluttering our bathroom." Piper grinned. "At least my husband knows I'm working hard."

"That you are," Meagan said.

Although Piper had been a well-respected investigative journalist for years, her career had shifted to beauty columnist not long ago, when the paper she worked for was bought out by a larger company. Now, her honest beauty product reviews and her courage to try what others were afraid to do made her a valuable contributor to her company and a favorite with her boss, Cooper Fox. She often brought her colorful stories to book club, and Meagan couldn't wait to hear how these next assignments would go.

Her hands finally free, Piper knelt and gave Hash Brown the attention he craved before she straightened to peer toward the back of the store. She waved to Nell, still on her chair, reading. "Is Nell hoarding the snacks?"

"Not at all," said Meagan. "Please, go and help yourself."

As Piper picked up her bags and made her way to the book club area, Olivia James and Avery Sheridan pushed open the bookshop door. They had both been part of the book club since its start, and despite their at-times hectic careers—Olivia as a nurse practitioner and Avery as a realtor and property manager—they made time most weeks to attend. Their heated conversation drew both Meagan's and Hattie's attention.

"No no no. Mr. Darcy beats Captain Wentworth every time. Best hero ever," Avery said.

"What?" Olivia's dark eyes narrowed, and she gave a derisive snort. "Darcy was clueless. Yes, he redeemed himself in the end, but Captain Wentworth was kind and sensitive."

"Until he thought Anne had cast him off." Avery propped her hands on her curvy hips, her long black hair spilling over her shoulders.

"Avery, Olivia, nice to see you today," Meagan said gently. "Discussing Jane Austen again?"

"Just her heroes," Avery said. She sniffed. "What smells so good?"

"Hazelnut coffee." Meagan made a note to bring the coffeepot from her office to the book club space in case people wanted more than one cup today. "Salted caramel syrup is there too, if that sounds good to you."

"That sounds fantastic," Olivia said before heading toward Nell, Piper, and the promise of a warm beverage.

Avery and Meagan followed, while Hattie went to guide a customer to the children's section.

As Avery found a seat, Meagan went to retrieve the coffeepot, and when she brought it to the snack table, Olivia held out an empty mug.

"Rough day?" Meagan asked, pouring the steaming brew into Olivia's cup.

Olivia scooped a spoonful of sugar into it. "Busy. With Nantucket heading into tourist season, we've had a fair number of new patients. Dr. Palmer is wondering if Island Family Medical Practice should open for a few hours on Saturdays."

Meagan winced. "I hope it doesn't come to that. You already stay so busy."

"That's the good thing about real estate," Avery cut in. "At least I can set my own hours, more or less."

Olivia smiled. "Being a nurse practitioner keeps me very busy, but it's good to know I'm helping people. I wouldn't trade it for anything."

"And that's why you're so good at it." Avery popped a piece of chocolate chip cookie into her mouth. "Mmm. Meagan, you are the master of sweet treats. You really should sell these. Along with your lemon cake."

Meagan placed a piece of that very cake on a paper plate and then found a chair between Piper and Nell. "I do enjoy baking, but a girl can't live on cookies and cake."

Avery laughed. "Speak for yourself."

As everyone settled in, Meagan picked up her copy of the book club book. Hash Brown had gotten comfortable next to her chair when the front door opened once more.

Luke's familiar form appeared. He chatted quietly with Hattie near the front counter for a few moments, then made his way over to them.

Olivia raised her eyebrows as she saw him walking their way. "Is that the lawyer from next door?"

"Yes." Meagan stood and called, "Hi, Luke." She then murmured to the women, "It will be nice to have a man in the club."

"A very handsome man," Avery said.

The women beamed and waved as Luke reached them.

An easy smile brightened his face. "Oh, good. I thought maybe I had the time wrong."

"Nope. We're just getting started," Meagan told him.

"Sorry I'm a few minutes late. Finishing up business with a client."

Hash Brown offered a happy yip, and Luke stooped to pet him. "I haven't forgotten about you, buddy."

Meagan smiled, watching Luke and Hash Brown. They made quite a pair.

Meagan shifted her attention to the others as Luke surveyed the snacks before taking a seat. She ignored the pointed looks her grandmother sent her way and quickly averted her gaze when Piper winked. *None of that.*

"So, Luke, tell us about yourself," Avery said as he sat down.

"There's not much to tell. My name is Luke Harris. I'm an attorney who likes history. I work next door to the bookshop. I moved here not long ago and am getting used to island life. So far, it's good."

Avery grinned. "Welcome. Hey, was that Honey Northcutt's car I saw in front of your building earlier?"

Luke hesitated. "Yes it was, though I'm not at leisure to tell you why she was there. Why do you ask?"

"You should know that Honey is a character," Avery explained. "She's sweet, spunky, but also particular. Her daughter, Alexis, is finicky as well. If you work with them, keep your wits about you."

He nodded. "Noted. Thank you."

"It's not like you to talk that way, Avery. Did you have a disagreement with them or something?" Piper asked.

Meagan tensed. Her friend could be blunt when she wanted information—sometimes too blunt.

Avery crossed her arms. "With Alexis, yes."

"What happened?" Clearly, Piper wouldn't let this go.

"Alexis hired me to sell her home, and when I couldn't do it quickly enough, her mother got on my case. Eventually, they fired me." She shook her head. "Alexis wanted the house sold in two *weeks*, which is nearly impossible in the housing business. You never know how long it's going to take. Sometimes you have three offers the first day, and other times a house can sit on the market for months. It simply depends on the house and the market, neither of which I have much control over." She shook her head as if ridding herself of unpleasant thoughts. "Anyway, enough about them."

Olivia took one hand off her coffee to pat Avery's arm. "I'm sorry you had to go through that, Avery."

"Losing a client is not easy, but it happens sometimes." Avery gave Meagan a sheepish grin. "I'm sorry. I didn't mean to derail the whole meeting."

"That's all right. I think we're all here, so we can focus on the book if everyone's ready." At the group's soft murmurs of agreement, Meagan smiled and flipped to the page she had marked. "So, has anyone not finished the book?"

No one raised their hand.

"In that case, what did you think of it? Did you like the way the story ended? Which characters did you connect with most?"

"Mmm." Piper swallowed a bite of lemon cake. "Charlotte."

"Okay. Why?"

"The poor girl loses everything and still keeps going."

Olivia shook her head. "I think Charlotte was a little too perfect. She never let herself grieve. She loses her mother and then her home in the war, and she simply pushes on? That doesn't seem believable to me. We hardly ever see her crack."

Piper frowned. "She does when Jack arrives. She doesn't trust him."

"What does that have to do with anything?"

"I think it might be a metaphor," Meagan suggested.

Everyone faced her, and she blushed at the sudden attention. "Think about it," she continued. "The enemy comes and burns not only her home but the entire valley to cinders. When Jack arrives, he becomes a symbol for all that has hurt her. Her loss. Death. Dreams."

"Well said, Meagan," Nell chimed in. "You did get your degree in library science, so you know a thing or two about making a point."

Conversations broke out about the book's secondary characters. Meagan turned to Luke. "Sorry for all the chatter. We're an enthusiastic bunch."

He grinned. "I'm enjoying it."

"I'm happy to hear that. Would you like to share your thoughts?"

"Sure."

The group quieted, apparently interested in his take.

Meagan said, "So, Luke, what do you think?"

Luke jumped right in. "To me, the story is about grief. Charlotte has to learn how to process hers, but Jack's arc is learning how to forgive himself. The tattoo branded on his arm clearly symbolizes that."

"Interesting," Meagan said. "But I think what the author was trying to say with the tattoo is that the past can't be undone. It marks us forever, whether good or bad. We can either try to hide it or learn from it."

"But that doesn't really tie into the overall theme of grief, does it?" Luke countered.

Meagan tilted her head. She hadn't expected Luke's challenge, but she found herself enjoying the chance to dig deeper into the purpose of the book. "They don't have to be mutually exclusive, do they?"

Luke's eyes widened. "You think the author was trying to convey multiple messages there?"

"The things that happen to us change the way we see the world." Meagan tried to steer the conversation back toward more neutral ground. "Charlotte can no longer trust men after the attack. Her heart is too bruised."

Luke rubbed his chin. "Yes. At least for a season. And isn't that the point? The story opens in the middle of a terrible difficulty. Yet we pray Charlotte doesn't stay stuck in her pain for long." He gazed down at his hands. "After I lost my wife, Jeanine, I thought life was over." He raised his head again with a small smile. "But now I see hope. Beauty in the hard places. And maybe the author of this book left it up to us to pick our own interpretation, because, like you said, the meanings of the metaphors don't have to be mutually exclusive."

"Touché," Piper said, taking the words out of Meagan's mouth.

Meagan shifted in her chair. Luke had really taken her by surprise. She liked that they could discuss different points of view in a mutually respectful way, and she was impressed that he'd analyzed the book so deeply.

Olivia raised her coffee cup. "Hard to beat that breakdown. Thanks, Luke."

"My pleasure."

Meagan tucked a strand of hair behind her ear. "Should we pick our next read?"

Piper snorted. "How about *War and Peace*?"

Meagan laughed.

Avery snapped her fingers. "I have an idea. How about that new mystery that's been climbing the best-seller charts? I can't remember the title."

"*The Stolen Witness*?" Nell asked.

"That's the one," Avery said.

Nell continued. "Maude, one of the ladies in Rotary Club, read it. She said it was great."

"What does everyone think?" asked Meagan. "Should we give it a try?" It didn't take long for the group to agree. "All right. Let's read the first few chapters by our next meeting. If you can't find a copy, let me know. We have plenty of them in stock here, if that helps."

As the group chatted, Luke helped Meagan throw away the paper plates and collect mugs. "Is it tradition to put new members on the spot to see if they have book club chops?" he teased.

Meagan bit her lip. "Sorry about that. And I'm so sorry about your wife. I didn't know."

Luke's playful expression dimmed. "Thank you. It happened four years ago. She was pregnant too." A shadow passed over him, and then he straightened. "I miss her and our baby, but I'm managing as best I can. The move has helped." He smiled. "This club is fun. Thank you for inviting me."

Meagan's heart ached for Luke's loss. "Anytime. And you're welcome back whenever. I appreciate your insight."

The two brought the dishes to the stockroom's large washtub and then rejoined the group near the front of the store. Meagan had decided the dishes could wait a few minutes.

Luke said goodbye to the women, then turned back to Meagan. "I'll try to join next week if my schedule allows it." Reaching down, he scratched Hash Brown's ears. "See you soon, Hash Brown."

Meagan grinned as the shop door closed. "That was fun, wasn't it?"

But she barely had spoken the words when the sound of sirens wailed in the distance. Meagan moved to the window, watching as an ambulance and a police car sped past in a blur. Luke paused at the door to his office too.

An ambulance is a strange sight on this tiny island. Meagan sent up a prayer that whoever needed help would get it, and soon.

3

Luke

Luke nodded as he closed the book on the prayers of George Washington. *A perfect way to start Sunday.* Crumpling up the wrapper that had housed his breakfast sandwich, he rose and tucked the book under his arm before waving goodbye to the staff at Aunt Maisie's. The servers at the diner smiled and called out their goodbyes. It was a nice place. He made a note to stop in for breakfast more often.

Stepping outside, he inhaled the cool ocean air drifting off the bay and stretched his legs before moving to grab his bike. The ride to church would do him good. The process of moving to Nantucket had left him without a regular exercise routine. Now, after a few weeks here, it was refreshing to be settled and finding his groove again.

He slid the book into his backpack next to his Bible and pedaled the few blocks to Trinity Christian Church, relishing the sun warming his shoulders. Nantucket's May weather was spoiling him. Rounding the last corner, he slowed and eased into the parking lot, quickly finding a spot to leave his bike and helmet during the service. Then he followed the other worshipers inside.

As he walked into the church foyer, he waved to a few familiar faces. He hadn't been in Nantucket long, but connections were starting to grow, and that warmed his heart.

"Good morning, Luke." Olivia crossed the space between them wearing a friendly smile. Her violet sweater complimented the dark tones of her skin and accentuated the honey-colored flecks in her brown eyes. "It's good to see you again. This is my husband, Kyle." She gestured to the man holding her hand.

Luke shook the tall man's free hand. "Nice to meet you."

"Likewise," Kyle said. "I hear you joined the Rose Cottage Book Club last week. Olivia said you really gave the group something to think about." His dark eyes danced. "I give her my thoughts all the time, but she isn't as appreciative of mine."

Olivia playfully swatted her husband's arm. "Oh, stop."

Luke chuckled at their good-natured teasing.

Olivia glanced toward the front of the sanctuary, and Luke followed her cue. The choir was assembling, their white robes swaying as they walked.

"We'll be starting soon," Olivia said. "Let's take our seats."

Kyle nodded. "Nice to meet you, Luke."

"Yes. Same to you, Kyle."

As the couple left him, Luke studied the crowded room and saw Meagan sitting a few pews away. She wore a soft, sage sundress and a cream-colored cardigan that accentuated her dark hair and blonde highlights.

A smile broke across her face when her gaze met his. Her hand lifted in a small wave. Returning the greeting, he stepped close and slid into the pew behind her.

"Good morning," he said.

"Morning." She twisted around in her seat. "I didn't know you attended church here."

"I haven't been for long, but I'm enjoying it. The people are so nice."

"Yes, they are. There's a Bible study on Wednesday at Piper's house if you're up for it."

"If I finish work on time, I'll try to come. Where does she live?"

"Mayhew Lane."

Tugging his phone from his pocket, he opened to his home screen. "Would you mind texting me her address?"

"Of course." She quickly messaged him, then faced forward again. The service was about to begin.

Luke turned his attention toward the white-robed choir, thankful for the friendships he was making in this place. As the singers lifted their voices in song and the congregation stood, he studied the large cross displayed on the vaulted wall—a place where both sorrow and joy met.

He bowed his head in prayer as the words of the song washed over him. *Lord, I feel like I'm at my own intersection. New beginnings after sorrow. Help me be the man You created me to be.*

Stella's and Honey's faces flashed through his mind. Different needs, different stories, yet they had come to him to share their load. *And help me be the servant You desire. I long to make a difference.*

Lifting his head, the lyrics fell from his lips as he joined in the song. "I surrender to Your will."

After church, Luke went home, made a turkey sandwich, and sat down to watch a television special on the Founding Fathers. But he didn't get to enjoy it long—his phone buzzed shortly after he pressed Play.

Wiping the crumbs from his fingers, he eyed his phone resting on the coffee table. A text message blinked on his screen.

Hey, I have a gift for you. Any chance you'll be near your office this afternoon? I know it's unusual for a Sunday.

He smiled. It was Meagan. Grabbing the phone, he typed, *Sure. Maybe around three?*

Several dots appeared as she typed.

Sounds good.

He settled back against the couch, warmth flooding his chest. It was nice to have a good neighbor like Meagan.

Right before three, he hopped on his bike and pedaled toward his office. The weather was warmer now, the morning's cooler air evaporating like a mist. Soon, he turned onto the road in front of his law office.

Meagan was waiting for him, holding a large green package with a giant golden bow on top.

He propped his bike against the building and met Meagan's sunny smile with a grin of his own. "Long time no see. You know, you don't have to bring a gift if you need legal counsel."

She shook her head. "No counsel needed. Consider it a belated 'welcome to the neighborhood' gift. Or we could call it a consolation prize for going toe-to-toe with a bookshop owner."

"I enjoyed it." He grinned and pointed at the package. "Avocado-print wrapping paper?"

She adjusted her thin-framed glasses. "I like funny stuff." She held the gift out so he could read the print on the paper—*Holy guacamole! It's a present.*

"How did you know I love avocados?" he joked. "Seriously, this is thoughtful of you."

Her smile widened. "It's not just from me, but from my grandmother too. Really, from everyone at Rose Cottage Books. We all look out for each other here."

"Of course." He smiled. "Why don't we go inside? I'll open it there."

"Sure."

Jiggling the keys in the lock, he let them in and flicked on the lights before setting the wrapped parcel on his desk.

"I hope you like it," Meagan said while he opened it.

After carefully tearing away the paper, Luke exclaimed in delight, running his fingers around the glossed edges of a picture frame. "My own copy of the Declaration of Independence." His gaze settled on Meagan, who stood near the windows with her head tilted slightly, the sun shining through her hair. "Thank you, Meagan. I love it. It'll go great in here."

Meagan grinned, then studied the walls around them, lingering on the Churchill painting. "I'm glad. You really do enjoy history."

"Yes. It's always been a passion of mine—books, artwork, quotes. I like them all, and I'm glad I have somewhere to display my small collection." He carried the new frame to an empty space on the wall and held it up for her to judge. "Here?"

"Perfect. Listen, I hope I didn't scare you off—at book club, I mean."

He laughed. "Not at all. I'm a lawyer. If I can't handle a spirited debate, I'm in the wrong profession."

She gave him a small smile. "I really did appreciate your thoughts—all of us did—and I hope you'll join us again."

"I will whenever I can manage."

Her smile grew. "Great. I'll let you get on with your day then. Enjoy."

"Thanks. And Meagan?"

Her brows lifted, waiting.

He paused. Being back in the office reminded him of his clients this past week. Honey had signed her will documents Friday, but Stella had been badgering him to visit Antonio at The Bad Punchline tonight. He realized now that he didn't want to go alone—and might not have to. "I was wondering if you wanted to go with me to The Bad Punchline comedy club tonight."

She hesitated. "Oh."

Not a particularly encouraging reply. "If you already have something going on, don't worry about it," he added quickly. "I just need to visit someone who works there, and it would be nice to have company. The book club members can come too if you want to invite them."

She smiled. "That sounds like fun."

"Have you ever been to a comedy club?"

"Once. I can see if any book club members are available. What time?"

"The show is at eight, so how about seven? We can chat beforehand."

"All right. The Bad Punchline. Seven o'clock."

"See you then."

He waited until she closed the door behind her before exhaling. He couldn't place what about Meagan rattled him. She was a neighbor, a friend. *A pretty friend.*

Shaking his head to free his thoughts, he retrieved from the file cabinet the manila folder holding Honey Northcutt's documents. He had yet to scan them. He might as well do something productive while he was here.

After taking care of the paperwork, he called Mrs. Northcutt to let her know everything was finished, but he got her voice mail. *Right. It's Sunday. She likely has much better things to do than sit around answering phone calls.* He was sure he would hear from her tomorrow.

Rising, he decided to head home before spending the evening searching for the not-so-funny truth behind Stella Jones's son-in-law.

Meagan

Meagan opened the door to her grandmother's house, barely containing an enthusiastic Hash Brown, who strained at the end of his leash. She laughed as she freed him. The walk around Sandpiper Park had given him energy rather than tired him out. With a happy yip, he raced off to find the bowl of water that Nell kept in the kitchen for him.

Meagan found her grandmother in the living room, reading the exotic fish guide she'd brought home last week. Meagan smiled when she noticed the fish tank tucked into the wall near where her grandmother sat. *Not long until you have company, little guys*, she mused.

"Hi, Nan. Hash Brown and I are back from our walk."

Her grandmother looked up and smiled. "I thought I saw him run by a second ago."

"He's on a water mission, I think. Which suddenly sounds like a great idea."

Meagan followed her dog into the kitchen to grab herself a bottle of water. She loved the room's dark cabinets, brown-and-black diamond-patterned flooring, welcoming windows, and modern appliances—a contrast to her own home's brighter, more classic tones.

Returning to the living room, she sat on one of the room's sofas and took a sip of water. "That little dog has so much fun at the park. If he were as big as Piper's dog, Ulysses, he'd really wear me out."

"Ah, he keeps you young." Nell folded her hands in her lap. "Perhaps I should get a dog."

Meagan studied the older woman affectionately. "Dog or no dog, you'll always be youthful in my eyes."

At Nell's laugh, Meagan grinned. "So, what are your plans tonight, Nan?"

"A group of friends invited me to play bingo."

"That sounds fun." Even at seventy-seven, her grandmother led a busy life. Meagan knew no matter where she went, her grandmother could make friends—and keep them for decades.

Nell waved her hand dismissively. "They're a sweet group, but I think I'll decline this time. I like spending my Sunday evenings puttering around in my garden. The weather is too lovely to stay cooped up inside. What about you? Going to get started on our next book club read?"

"Um, no. I have plans, actually." Meagan shot her a sidelong glance. "I'm going to The Bad Punchline comedy club."

"Oh?" Nell's brows lifted. "You've never mentioned going there before. By yourself?"

"No. Luke invited me." While the thought was fresh in her mind, she sent a group text to the other book club members, inviting them.

Nell smiled. "I thought I smelled something brewing between you two at book club."

"Nan, behave." Meagan needed to nip her grandmother's matchmaking ways in the bud, as she had with Hattie. Besides, Luke had lost his wife and child. Dating was surely the last thing on his mind.

She fixed Nell with a mock glare and crossed her arms. "I wasn't the only one he invited. Luke said the whole book club could come. That includes you. He made it very clear it wasn't a date. Stop scheming."

Nell gave her a too-innocent expression. "Now can I help it if I see what's obvious?" She shook her head. "Anyway, I have no interest in going to a comedy club, dear. If the others want to join, that's fine, but I'll stay home and happily tend my mayflowers and violets.

And yes, take care of Hash Brown too."

At the sound of his name, Hash Brown bounced into the room, his ears alert, as if someone had suggested a treat for him.

"But no digging up my flowers this time, young man. You hear?"

Hash Brown barked and danced in a circle, his little body wiggling with excitement.

Just then Meagan's phone rang.

"Hi, Meagan," Olivia's voice chirped on the other end.

"Hi, Olivia. How are you? Are you calling about going to the comedy club tonight?"

"I got your text, but I can't go. Kyle and I have plans, but thank you for inviting us. I'm actually calling to make sure everything's okay at the bookshop."

Meagan blinked in surprise. The shop was closed on Sundays. What could be wrong? "I believe so. Why do you ask?"

"Kyle and I just heard there were a couple of break-ins a few blocks over last night, and he thought we should check in with you."

Fear prickled Meagan. *Break-ins?* Forcing a confident tone into her voice, she said, "I was around there earlier and everything seemed okay, but thank you for letting me know."

"Anytime. You know Kyle. Security is a way of life for that man. The joys of working in cybersecurity."

Meagan nodded as though her friend could see her. "Do you mind me asking who was robbed?"

At the word *robbed*, Nell sat up, concern etched on her face.

"It's okay, Nan," Meagan assured her. "I'll fill you in later."

The woman eased slowly back against her sofa cushions, keeping a sharp eye on her granddaughter.

"Sea Breeze Yarns. It was the strangest thing, though." Olivia paused as if she were considering her next words, and Meagan's heart raced as she waited. "When I talked to Judith about it, she said the money was still in the register. Petty cash was all accounted for. The thief tore apart a bunch of balls of yarn and strung them all over the store."

"What?" Meagan shook her head. "That doesn't make sense. Wouldn't that make it vandalism then?"

"I suppose the police could classify it as that, except some of the yarn was found outside the back door. With all the mess, Judith is having a hard time figuring out exactly how much yarn was taken or destroyed."

Meagan frowned. Judith Pappoulos, who owned the yarn shop, wasn't easy to confuse. "So strange."

Olivia sighed. "Who on earth would rob that place? Judith is one of the sweetest women on the island."

"I have no idea, but that is upsetting." Meagan's eyes settled on Nell. "I suppose we'll have to be more diligent at the store. Do you think I should get a security system?"

"It's not a bad idea, but I would wait and see what the police say after they've investigated."

Still, Meagan resolved to go over to the shop right after their conversation to check on the building. The thought of alerting Larry Krump, her landlord, also crossed her mind, but she decided against it. The man was known for his nervous disposition and didn't need unfounded worries crowding his mind. She'd tell him if they discovered that there was a problem to worry about. "Sounds good."

"Have a good night, Meagan. And sorry if I scared you. I'm sure the police are on it. Enjoy the comedy club."

"Thank you, Olivia. And thank Kyle for me. I'll let you know how everything goes."

After hanging up, Meagan briefly recounted the story to Nell, who agreed Meagan should stop at Rose Cottage Books. She hurried to the shop on her bicycle. The sight of the store's pink shingled exterior warmed her like a ray of sunshine as usual, but this time it also awakened a feeling of tenderness. What if her beloved shop had also come under attack?

Hattie and her husband, John, met her there, and together they conducted a thorough check inside and out. Nothing was amiss, it appeared. Meagan relaxed on her ride home, taking comfort in the fact that she could enjoy her evening without worrying too much.

Back at Nell's house, Meagan and Nell enjoyed a nice dinner of pot roast and mashed potatoes together, then Meagan helped her grandmother clean up before bidding her a good night.

But Nell stopped her at the door with a flood of questions. "What will you wear? A cute dress maybe? Will you curl your hair?"

Meagan had debated this very thing but ultimately settled on comfortable, casual attire. *Something I'd wear on any nice evening.* "I have some ideas. I'll come back with Hash Brown before I leave."

"Very well, dear. See you soon."

As she and Hash Brown crossed the courtyard, Meagan brooded—not about the evening ahead, but about Olivia's phone call and what that could mean. The break-in at Sea Breeze Yarns bothered her. *Sirens the other night, reports of theft today. What is going on in Nantucket?*

Luke

Luke toyed with the straw in his ginger ale and let his gaze roam the crowded comedy club. Couples chatted at small circular tables. Friends huddled in conversation as they munched appetizers in front of the small stage. The clink of glasses, the trill of laughter, and the hum of the sound system created an excitement that rippled through the air. He waved, spying Meagan and Piper winding their way between the tables. Meagan wore jeans and a crimson blouse, while Piper was dressed in a flowy black gown with billowing sleeves. Everything about them looked relaxed and graceful.

He greeted them, then called the waitress over to get their drink and snack orders.

Piper glanced at the menu, her chin lifting slightly as she read. "Fried pickles? Those are my favorite." To the waitress she said, "I'll take one order of those with a cherry soda, please." Then to her friends she murmured, "I'm going to need a roll of antacids before the night is over."

They all chuckled.

The waitress turned to Meagan. "And for you, miss?"

"I'd like a hot fudge sundae with extra hot fudge, please."

"You got it."

Luke arched a brow. "Sweet tooth?"

Meagan lifted her chin. "One does not resist chocolate."

He smiled and asked the waitress for potato skins as well.

"There goes my healthy-eating streak," Meagan teased.

"It's nice to enjoy yourself every once in a while." Luke winked. "And the check is on me tonight, ladies. Thanks for coming. Believe it or not, this is research, and it's a lot more enjoyable to share it with someone. I'm sorry the others couldn't make it."

"Yeah, Avery had something come up at work, and Olivia and Kyle had already planned a date by themselves," said Meagan.

"That's too bad," Piper said. "But at least we will have a good time."

Moments later, the waitress returned with their order.

"Thanks," Piper said as she eagerly dug into her fried pickles. She ate one, then asked Meagan, "So Nell couldn't come tonight?"

Meagan shook her head. "She wanted to work in her garden. Besides, Hash Brown provides enough laughs for any evening. When I left, he was busy sniffing around the yard, trying to make friends with squirrels."

Luke smiled. "He's certainly entertaining."

"That he is." Meagan stuck her spoon into her sundae. "You said this visit is for research. Can you elaborate?"

He shook his head. "Not much, I'm afraid. A new client is having me look into something."

"Funny place for research," Piper said with a wink. "Get it? Funny place? It's a comedy club?"

Luke and Meagan laughed.

"Speaking of work," Piper continued, "I wish I could cover more than cosmetics for the magazine. It's fun and all—and I do enjoy writing a good, honest review—but lots of other topics interest me. For instance, this club. I'd love to profile some of the comics, or perhaps the club itself as a busy night spot in Nantucket. I'm not sure Cooper would go for it, though—too touristy and not a great fit for the department." She licked her lips. "One thing I do know—I can recommend the fried pickles if anyone asks."

Overhead, the lights dimmed and a booming voice drew their attention to the stage. "Ladies and gentlemen, The Bad Punchline is pleased to present Antonio Poppalardo!"

The announcer drew out the comic's name as the crowd burst into cheers. Luke's focus narrowed to the dark-headed man who sauntered on stage and grabbed the mic from the stand. He wore dark jeans, a Batman T-shirt, and a sports coat.

A relaxed vibe, Luke noted.

"Thanks, guys. Yeah, you heard that right. My name is Poppalardo. Yes, I have heard every possible pronunciation of my name. Boy, did the other kids give me grief in elementary school."

Laughter rippled around the room, but Luke wasn't among them. He set his phone on the edge of the table before starting the voice recorder app.

"Poppalardo is Italian. Ah, Italy. The land of spaghetti." The comic's eyes twinkled. "When I married into my wife's family, my mother-in-law thought that was all I would eat—pasta and pizza. But the problem with Italian food is that five or six days later, you're hungry again."

The crowd responded, and Luke crossed his arms. Sure, Antonio had mentioned his mother-in-law, but there had been nothing negative about her in the statement. Maybe the jokes he'd seen on the Internet were a one-time event.

Antonio paced across the stage. "That's something I was not prepared for—the mother-in-law. You know what I mean? This guy in the front here sure does, don't you, buddy?" As the audience hooted, he chuckled. "Ah, actually mine isn't so bad. My wife and I named our daughter after her. Anxious Annie turns five next week."

The room erupted with more bellows of amusement. Piper's brows lifted. Meagan frowned as Luke winced. That joke was a bit more personal. However, as long as he didn't mention the woman's name—

"In all honesty, my mother-in-law's name is Stella."

Luke groaned under his breath. *So much for anonymity.*

"I always know when Stella starts knocking at my front door because the mice start throwing themselves on the traps."

Unease crawled up Luke's spine as everyone in the room—except Luke, Meagan, and Piper—burst into laughter. He shifted. This wasn't good. Beside him, Meagan and Piper wore expressions of discomfort that he was sure matched his own.

Antonio let the crowd quiet down, then continued. "Speaking of animals, did you hear about the man who threw his mother-in-law into the lion's den at the zoo? He's being sued by a wildlife protection group for cruelty to animals."

At the applause, Antonio bowed and waved. "That's all for me tonight. You've been a fabulous audience. Thank you and good night!"

Luke stopped the recording on his phone. Nearly the entire set had been aimed at Stella, or at least mother-in-law material. He blew out a breath. *Are all of Antonio's comedy gigs like this? If so, convincing him to change his whole act won't be easy.*

"That was different." Piper's words mirrored Luke's turbulent thoughts.

"You okay?" Meagan asked him quietly.

Luke forced himself to smile. "Yes. I was deep in thought about something."

"The case you're working on?"

He took a drink of his ginger ale. "Yes."

Piper straightened. "Doesn't the poster outside say the next comic is a woman?"

"I think so."

"Let's hope she's better than that guy was. He got a lot of laughs, but I can't say I enjoyed his material." She motioned to Meagan. "Come with me to the bathroom. I want to show you a new product I'm testing. They call it glitter dust. To you and me, it's shiny eyeshadow."

Meagan smiled. "All right. You sure you're okay, Luke?"

"I'm fine."

But by the way she looked at him, he knew he hadn't fooled her.

He twisted in his seat to study the rest of the room. Antonio stood at the back, signing autographs. Luke realized he could go directly to the source himself rather than simply observing him. This was the perfect opportunity to connect. Not as a defendant and lawyer, but as one person to another.

Striding across the club, Luke approached as the last admirer left. He offered his hand with a smile.

"Mr. Poppalardo? Luke Harris. Great stuff tonight."

Antonio shook Luke's hand gladly. "Thanks, man. I'm happy you enjoyed it."

"Do you have a minute?" Luke gestured toward an empty table in the back of the club.

"Sure." Once seated, Antonio waved toward a waiter, motioned for a bottle of water, then turned back to Luke. "I'm always so thirsty after these things."

"How many times do you perform in a week?"

"It depends. This week my agent has me booked for Sunday, Tuesday, and Thursday. It varies. Sometimes it's a five-minute set. Other times it's twenty. The longest set I've put together is forty." He shook his head then took a bottle of water a waiter offered to him. "That one was exhausting."

"I bet. Do you write new material each time?"

"Some. The themes don't really change, but I try not to tell the same jokes." A small smile curved his lips. "The regulars would notice pretty quickly."

Luke propped his elbows on the table. "I recently picked up a comedy-writing book. I had no idea so much was involved in the craft of stand-up."

"It can be pretty intense." Antonio took a sip of his water and relaxed against the wooden chair. "The rule of three, repetition, misdirection, refining the jokes themselves—all that stuff takes years of working out and grinding away. And timing the laughs at regular intervals? That's an art form all its own. But if you've got the drive, you can master it."

Luke had to hand it to the man—he seemed like someone who put his all into his craft. "So, what got you into comedy? The love of laughter?"

"Nah. Comedy is more than that. Most people are surprised to learn the majority of comics are deep thinkers. We're a pretty quiet group in our everyday lives. Too busy observing the world around us to be clowning nonstop. What we really do is expose the truth and maybe process it ourselves as we do. We poke holes in fears and hopes and dreams and even societal constructs to see if we can inspire a laugh. It's a tough gig." His brows lowered as he traced a scar in the table with his finger. "I like to think of it as a combination of speaking truth and giving laughter. With a little touch of free therapy, because things don't seem as bad if you can laugh at them."

"I usually hear it phrased 'getting laughs' rather than 'giving laughter.'"

"Nah, getting laughs is centered on self. But *giving* laughter?" Antonio smiled. "That's focusing on everyone else. There's nothing better. Laughter is a great way to cope with hard times. It's something I can do to help people."

Luke grinned. "Like medicine."

"Just call me Dr. Poppalardo."

This man wasn't at all who Luke had assumed him to be. "Is comedy all you do? I mean, is it a full-time job?"

Antonio rolled the lid of his water bottle between his thumb and finger. "I'd like it to be, but no. The life of a stand-up comic doesn't pay much. I'm a teacher. I do comedy mostly in the summer."

"Wow. I wouldn't have guessed that." Luke smiled. "Do you enjoy teaching?"

Antonio pursed his lips. "Most of the time, yes. The students can be a handful, but it takes a sense of humor to deal with them. Still, getting to pour knowledge into the next generation and watch them flourish under kindness is awesome work."

Luke studied the man across from him. Thoughtful. Intelligent. Nothing about Antonio or his beliefs matched the portrait Stella had painted. Still, his jokes caused the woman grief. There had to be a way to help this family.

"Sounds like you have a wonderful life." Luke leaned back in his chair. "I'd love to talk with you more in the future. If I contact you again, would you mind letting me pick your brain about your approach a bit?"

"Sure. I'm still learning myself, but I'm always happy to help." Antonio tugged his wallet from his back pocket and handed Luke a business card. "Call anytime."

"Thanks." Luke rose and stretched out his hand. "It's been good talking with you."

"Likewise," said Antonio.

Luke was deep in thought as he wove between the empty tables back to his friends. He and Antonio had gotten off on the right foot. At least that would make the prospect of mediation easier.

He scanned the area as he approached the table. Piper and Meagan were still gone. Flickering lights told him the next act would begin soon, so he imagined they'd return momentarily. He lowered himself into his seat and drummed his fingers on the table.

Then he remembered. He never had talked to Honey. He supposed he could try one more time to reach her while he waited. He found her number in his phone and tapped the Call button. One ring. Two. Three.

"Hello?"

Luke stilled. The answering voice sounded too young to belong to Honey. "Hello. May I speak to Honey Northcutt?"

"Oh." The voice wobbled, and he heard sniffling. "I'm Honey's daughter, Alexis."

"Forgive me, Alexis. I'm your mother's attorney, Luke Harris. I need to speak with her."

He heard Alexis suck in a deep breath before she replied, "Haven't you heard? My mother is dead."

Piper

Piper shifted the two small shopping bags in her hand as she stood in front of Rose Cottage Books and pushed the door open. A bell jingled overhead, and from somewhere near the back, Hash Brown released a series of excited barks.

She smiled. With Meagan's help, she could change last week's secret-shopping experience from a burden to a blessing.

Meagan rounded the shelf of new releases, Hash Brown on her heels. "You're here early." Her gaze dropped to the bags Piper held and then lifted again. "More shopping?"

"Nope. Leftovers from last week." Piper knelt as Hash Brown bounded forward to greet her. She stroked his soft fur and looked up at Meagan. "I'm here because I could use your help."

Meagan shook her head. "No, you can't color my hair."

"I promise it's nothing as wild as that." Piper rose, shifting her bags and opening them for Meagan to inspect.

"Good."

"Cooper wants me to write the secret-shopper article, giving store ratings, recommendations, warnings—all that stuff—but he also wants me to test a few products on someone other than me for a change. To get another perspective." She grinned, then mustered her best pleading expression.

Meagan propped one hand on her hip. "Why do I get the feeling you've picked me?"

Piper laughed and moved toward the restroom. "Do you have a minute?"

Meagan sighed and inclined her head, motioning to Hattie to take over the register. "Okay, this once. But try not to make me into one of your beauty product mishaps." It was well known that since taking the beauty columnist role, Piper had had her fair share of surprises on the job.

"Scout's honor."

She and Meagan paraded to the small bathroom, located in the stockroom, while Hash Brown waited outside. Piper spread the cosmetics across the counter, then tossed the empty bags aside. Lip glosses, mascara tubes, and eyeshadow boxes spilled onto the small vanity. "Most of these are from a fairly new cosmetic line called Blossom Inc."

Meagan eyed them warily, as if they might bite. "I see. But why do you need me? Couldn't Avery or Olivia help?"

Piper waved her hand. "You know that Olivia is low-key when it comes to cosmetics, and Avery only wears that high-dollar, froufrou stuff on special occasions. You, though, are the sort of person to help in a pinch—and your makeup game isn't bad either. Subtle, but done well." She whirled and studied Meagan's face carefully. "Hmm. Your coloring is a cross between a cool winter and a warm autumn." She reached for a box of eyeshadow and shook it. "It'll be fun. We'll probably discover techniques that don't work for you, but we might also stumble across something that does. You in? I'll be experimenting on myself too if it makes you feel better."

Meagan grinned. "Anything for a friend."

The two of them giggled as they applied the products one by one, discussing the merits and drawbacks of each, and marveling at their ability to accentuate various features. When Piper offered Meagan a tube of bright-red lipstick, her friend held up a hand. "Absolutely not. It's the wrong color for me. I do subtle, remember?"

"It's part of the research," Piper said. "You already have winged eyeliner and a smoky eye. This will go perfectly with that, and it might even become your new signature shade. If you don't like it, you can wipe it off. Besides, you've trusted me this far. Would I let you down now?"

Meagan wrinkled her nose but gave in. "Fine."

Piper handed her the tube of lipstick before grabbing some bronzing powder. "My skin is too fair for this. It might work on you, though." She shot Meagan a glance, watching her apply the powder next. "The comedy club last night was fun. The first comic wasn't my cup of tea, but I enjoyed the others."

"Me too." Meagan studied her red lips in the mirror. Piper hid a smug smile. Her friend wore the color well. "Although Luke looked less than impressed the whole night."

Piper opened a small box and laughed before holding it up for Meagan's inspection. "Fake eyelashes."

Meagan studied them with open apprehension. "Never used those before."

"Me neither. We'll conquer them together." Piper handed her some to try on before she leaned toward the mirror to painstakingly apply her own. "Yeah. I was surprised when Luke finally told us what bothered him, even if he couldn't reveal the person's name."

"Yes," Meagan said. "I can't imagine how that might feel—to lose a client so soon after meeting them. A shame."

"Yes," Piper said. "Listen, even though Luke couldn't tell us, I think I figured out who his client is—was."

Meagan paused in her application of the first lash strip. "And why do you think that?"

Piper pulled out her phone, unlocked it, and showed Meagan what was on the screen. "A little peek at the *Dolphin Gazette*'s obituaries tells me that freshly added to the list is Mrs. Honey Northcutt."

Meagan gasped. "Isn't that who Avery was talking about at book club?"

"One and the same."

"Poor Luke." Meagan frowned at her reflection. "I met the woman a few times, once at Pirate Treasures Candy and another at Young's Farm." She glanced at Piper. "I never really got to know her personally, but she seemed nice. She came off as kind and outgoing. I never saw her in the bookshop, so I'm guessing she wasn't much of a reader. I feel bad that she passed, but honestly, I'm more worried about Luke. He seemed upset all night."

"I got the same impression," Piper said. "Is he planning to come to Bible study at our house on Wednesday? Maybe that will help him."

"I'm not sure. He sounded excited when I invited him yesterday, but he did say it would depend on his workload."

"Hopefully he'll be there." Piper studied Meagan's appearance and reached for a tube of light-pink gloss for herself. "And imagine his delight when the makeover model Meagan Poe enters the room."

Meagan rolled her eyes. "You're as bad as Hattie and Nan."

Piper smiled, her oversize lashes emphasizing her amusement. "Don't worry. I won't push you about it." She yelped. "Oh, how could I forget?"

"What?" Meagan whirled toward her, an eyebrow pencil in hand.

"A number of Nantucket businesses were robbed last night."

"No, it was the day before yesterday," Meagan countered. "Sea Breeze Yarns, for one."

Piper winced. "More were hit last night, sadly. The library and Farmhouse Chic."

"Goodness. What's going on? I haven't lived on Nantucket very long, but I've never heard of anything like this happening before now."

"Yes, it's super rare here." Piper patted her arm. "The police are on it.

I'm sure of that. Don't let it worry you. I'm sure it'll be resolved quickly."

Meagan's nod told Piper she only half believed her. "I was talking with Olivia about putting in a security system. Is that too hasty?"

"It might be a good idea," Piper said as she admired herself in the mirror. She hadn't meant to ruin the fun they'd been having. *Time to change the subject.* "Wow. This is a great lip gloss. I'll be giving it a stellar review."

"It does seem good."

Piper tapped her chin. "Of course, the best way to give a thorough review is to see how well it lasts." She smiled. "Guess I'll be wearing this stuff out of here. What about you?"

Meagan tugged a makeup wipe from a pack on the counter. "I don't think so. The bright red lipstick and fake eyelashes are too much for me. They might scare my customers."

Piper laughed. "Fair enough." She began piling the cosmetic buffet back into her shopping bags. "About the break-ins, stay alert, but don't stress too much. Talk to your landlord if you need backup or want to run the security system by him. Or put Luke on security duty. I'm sure he can handle anyone with that athletic build of his." They both giggled at the thought. "It'll be fine."

"It will," Meagan answered.

"By the way, did you hear from Avery about her work meeting last night?"

"She texted late last night. It wasn't a meeting—it was a date." Piper's eyes widened. "Oh."

"She said it didn't go as well as she'd hoped, though."

"That's too bad. What happened?"

Meagan grimaced. "They met at a restaurant and everything started out fine, but when she returned from a quick trip to the restroom, she caught him flirting with a woman seated in the next booth."

"I assume that means she isn't going to see him again."

"Never."

"Bummer. A good guy is out there for her. They just haven't found each other yet."

"I pray it's sooner rather than later, for Avery's sake." Meagan faced Piper and struck a pose. "What do you think?"

"Beautiful, as always." She smiled at Meagan, thankful for the friendship that had quickly developed between them. "Are you sure you don't want that blazing-red lipstick? It looked great on you."

Tucking the makeup back into one of the bags, Meagan shook her head. "I'll pass."

"And here I thought we were going to make a statement," Piper teased.

"Oh, I would make a statement all right." Meagan pulled a paper towel from the dispenser and wiped up the powder that peppered the countertop. "Have you started the new book club book yet?"

"I love it. Sucked me right in."

"Me too." Meagan tossed the paper towel into the trash can. "But can you imagine living in a place with so much turmoil? That grungy, dystopian kind of gloomy existence?"

Piper paused for a moment and then shook her head. "Never. We've been spoiled in Nantucket. I think I'm suffering when the market is out of pomegranates."

Meagan laughed. "Do you have enough feedback to write a thorough review?"

Tossing a highlighter and mascara into the last bag, Piper nodded. "I believe so. Thanks again for your help."

"It was fun." Meagan opened the door. "Next time we'll have to get Hattie in on it."

"Deal."

Meagan followed Piper out of the bathroom. Hash Brown padded two steps behind them back to the counter, glad to have his human in sight.

Piper waved goodbye to her friend and stepped outside into the brisk air. As she slid behind the steering wheel, she paused. Her lips were tingling. She lowered the visor to see her reflection in the overhead mirror. Her lips were definitely fuller. *Isn't that what lip-plumping gloss does?*

She started the car and pushed the visor back into position. Her lips weren't just tingling now. They were burning.

Pawing through the bag of cosmetics in the passenger seat, she found the lip-plumping gloss and studied the warnings. *May cause slight tingling.*

Maybe this was normal and she simply wasn't used to it.

She headed down the street, her lips growing fuller and more painful with each passing second. She needed to do something. At the next light, she pulled to a stop and touched her lips. They had doubled in size. She quickly wiped off the gloss with a napkin she found in her car, but the tingling persisted.

Spying a fast-food restaurant up ahead, she whipped into the drive-thru and ordered a large cup of ice. Once she'd received the cup, she popped off the lid and pressed the frozen chunks to her mouth.

Relief.

When she arrived home she dashed into the house, calling for Jim.

He appeared and shook his head at the sight of her. "Another beauty blunder?" Without waiting for an answer, he went to fetch some allergy medicine.

Meanwhile, Piper made a beeline to the bathroom and studied her puffy mouth. Her lips had plumped all right—or rather, they'd ballooned.

With Jim's help and a few ice packs to reduce swelling, Piper's discomfort started to subside. Settling into her living room chair later, ice packs on her lips, she had to chuckle. *Of course I'd have a reaction.*

But that's the joy of the job, right? She knew that no matter what happened, it was all material for her article. Cooper and the readers wanted to know it all—the good, the bad, and the miserable.

Luke

Luke adjusted his tie as he examined the massive front door of Honey Northcutt's home. Its dark-green color reminded him of Christmas. A bronze door knocker loomed in the top center, under a peephole. When he'd called Honey and Alexis had answered, he'd never imagined he'd be visiting the Northcutt mansion the next day. Alexis had been insistent, however, so he'd agreed to stop by.

The three-story house made him think of a chic fortress, complete with a whitewashed shingled exterior, wide-paneled windows, a bubbling fountain, oversize hedges, and white columns. All of it emphasized Honey's obvious wealth.

He cleared his throat and knocked.

The door opened to reveal a middle-aged woman with mascara-streaked eyes. Her bleach-blonde hair was tousled, yet despite her disheveled appearance, she wore pristine cream capris and a lime-green silk blouse. Bracelets dangled from her wrists and clinked against each other as she dabbed a tissue to her nose.

"Hello. I'm Luke Harris, Mrs. Northcutt's attorney."

"Mr. Harris." The woman sniffled. "I'm Alexis. Thank you so much for coming over. I was so grateful for your call last night."

"Thank you for inviting me here. It's nice to meet you, Alexis. Please accept my condolences. Your mother seemed like a wonderful person."

At the mention of Honey, the woman whimpered into her tissue. "My poor mother." She blew her nose and waved him inside. "Please, come in."

"Thank you. I only wish I were here under better circumstances."

She swiped away the smeared mascara under her eyes. "Yes. Everything happened so sudden. It seems like only yesterday we were together." She offered a smile that didn't reach her eyes. "She loved to buy me clothes and take me to fancy restaurants. Now what will I do without her?"

Luke moved to pat her shoulder, but Alexis's phone rang. Strains of electronic pop filled the air as she pulled the phone from her pocket. She checked the screen and groaned. "It's my uncle. He's been persistent, wanting to know the details for Mother's funeral." She offered an apologetic smile as she silenced the device. "I haven't gotten that far yet. It's only been two days, and no one's offered to help me. Why does everything fall on me?" She jammed the phone back into her pocket. "I was going to vacay in Florida this week, but does anyone care? No."

Luke blinked. Was there ever a convenient time to die? It wasn't as if Honey had planned to pass away. He forced his features to remain impassive as Alexis released a wail, pressing the tissue to her eyes.

"What I wouldn't give for one of Mother's shopping trips. We always had the best time."

"I'm sure this must be difficult," Luke said, not missing the fact that so far, Alexis's main regret sounded like the loss of her mother's spoiling her, rather than the loss of the woman herself. But he knew grief did strange things to people. It might be easier for Alexis to focus on an inconsequential loss rather than the main one right now.

"You don't even know." She sniffed. "You couldn't possibly have any idea."

Luke looked away. No, he wouldn't understand. He'd merely buried his wife and unborn child four years ago. Pursing his lips, he followed Honey's distraught daughter into the spacious living room. Its tall windows flooded the space with sunshine. He glanced from wall to wall, taking in the honey-colored hardwood floors, white sofas, marble vases overflowing with fake flowers, and a large Oriental rug beneath the furniture. He fought the urge to check his shoes for mud. Everything was polished like a museum, throwing off warmth, but somehow it wasn't as inviting as he would have expected from the woman he'd met a few days ago.

Alexis took a seat on the overstuffed sofa across from him. "Mother loved antiques anywhere she could put them. Those vases? Her pride and joy from the eighteenth century." Her bottom lip started to quiver.

Luke shifted his gaze, giving the woman privacy in her grief.

"I appreciate you coming over," Alexis continued, her sadness vanishing as quickly as it had appeared. "I suppose I need to know how much it will cost to bury her."

Easing onto the edge of the immaculate sofa, Luke glanced her way again. "I'm sorry, but I'm not sure. Funeral homes set the price for burials and services. I can only discuss issues relating to your mother's will."

Alexis's eyes lit up at that. "That's so kind of you. What did she leave? Assets, stocks, bonds, accounts?"

Luke folded his hands together, wishing for a mug of coffee or a cup of tea to make the place feel warmer. "To start, Alexis, you should know that your mother had me change her will right before her death."

Silence grew as the color left the woman's face. "What? Why?" Alexis bit her lip.

"She said she wanted to include you and your brother in it."

Alexis bowed her head, a faint smile spreading over her face. "That makes me happy, Mr. Harris. What did she leave me?"

"There will be a reading of the will soon, but first I—"

Alexis rose and paced around the room. "Can't we skip that part? Surely I can act as her power of attorney. I should be able to know what she left me right now, shouldn't I?"

"Power of attorney is no longer valid after death," Luke explained. "The only person who can act on behalf of the deceased is the representative filed through the court. That would be me. There's a process that must happen before you know the details of your mother's wishes."

"I don't believe this." Alexis propped her hands on her hips, her nostrils flaring.

Luke rose, keeping his voice calm and even. "I promise everything will be processed in the normal manner. Once any outstanding debts are paid, the probate court will contact all those mentioned as your mother's beneficiaries. That includes you."

"Fine. But she did leave me her estate, right, Mr. Harris?"

"I can't say anything until the court hearing."

"When will that be?" She shot him a piercing stare, though it lost some of the effect when coupled with her smeared makeup and red eyes. "Tomorrow or the next day?"

He shook his head. "No. Likely within a few weeks."

"Oh." She plopped back into the plush furniture. "That's a shame. It would be so wonderful to have everything settled and finished."

Luke shifted. Alexis was far too eager to view her mother's accounts. Most families he encountered were shocked at their loved one's passing, unable to process things like the details of the estate. Alexis seemed to thrive on the news of her impending financial increase.

He had opened his mouth to reply when the front door burst open. A tall, thin man with salt-and-pepper hair barged in.

"You answer my calls, young lady," he snapped. He stopped in front of Alexis, flushed with anger.

She smirked. "Hello, Victor. Nice day for a visit, isn't it?"

"Don't you sass me. It's high time we settled this."

Settled what? Luke leaned in, listening closely.

Alexis waved a hand toward Luke, her smile smug. "By all means.

This is Mother's attorney, Mr. Harris."

Luke extended a hand. "Nice to make your acquaintance."

"We were discussing Mother's will," Alexis said.

"Really?" The man's gaze swiveled to Luke as he took the hand offered to him. "Victor Northcutt, Honey's brother-in-law."

"Mr. Northcutt, it's a pleasure."

Victor chuckled. "You have far better manners than my niece here. I'm trying to assemble a family meeting to discuss my sister-in-law's funeral and estate."

Luke stuffed his hands in his pockets. "Yes sir. Honey recently hired me as her legal representative, and her estate will likely be settled in the next few weeks."

Victor's eyes narrowed. "I pray Honey used good sense. Do you know my late brother left everything—*everything*—to Honey when he kicked the bucket? Didn't give one red cent to his family." He scowled. "No gratitude for those of us who supported him in his lean times before he found success. Did you know he once borrowed five thousand dollars from me to start a business? He never did pay me back. Honey wouldn't let him."

Luke shook his head. "No, I didn't know that."

"My brother is gone, but I'll have plenty to say if she left me high and dry like her husband did. She knew full well how much I've helped her through rough spots, and I deserve my due." Then he smiled. "But we talked it all out, she and I, a while back, and I know it'll all work out how it's meant to."

Alexis stood, lifting her chin as she studied her uncle. "Are you kidding? You've been nothing but a pain to Mother for years. There's no way she'd—"

Luke stepped between them. "I'm sorry, but this fighting is unnecessary. Mr. Northcutt, with all due respect, you have no idea of the contents in

Honey's will. She had me change it not long before her death."

Both of them hushed, and Victor glared at him. "What is this? Some kind of trickery on her part?" His eyes glittered. "Or perhaps some fancy maneuvering of yours, *lawyer*."

Luke took a breath to steady his emotions. "As I told Alexis shortly before your arrival, the probate court will contact all involved parties once everything has been processed. Until then, please call if you need my legal services." He pulled a business card from his wallet and handed it to Alexis.

Before either of them could respond, the doorbell rang. Alexis muttered, "Now what?" She opened the door, and her irritation melted into delight. "DeeDee, how kind of you to come."

An older woman bearing a covered pie entered. She wore navy slacks, black loafers, a cream blouse, and a friendly smile on her plump face. "Now, you know you couldn't keep me away, sweetie." She set the dessert on an end table and wrapped the younger woman in a hug. "I've found there's not much that apple pie can't cure."

"Thank you. I love your apple pie." Alexis wiped tears from her eyes and turned to make introductions. "DeeDee, this is Mr. Harris, and you know my uncle Victor. Mr. Harris, this is DeeDee Davis." She smiled. "She and my mother were best friends."

DeeDee, thought Luke. *She was written into Honey's new will.* He stepped forward. "Mrs. Davis. I'm Honey's attorney."

She waved her hand as if shooing him. "Now, none of that 'Mrs. Davis' talk. I'm plain old DeeDee." She swept her gaze over Alexis. "How are you holding up, dear?"

"It's so hard." Tears spilled down Alexis's cheeks once more. "It's a strange thing. Those who aren't close to you appear and offer a helping hand." She shot a glare at Victor. "Then others you thought you could count on vanish." She sniffed. "Kevin has yet to stop in."

DeeDee clucked her tongue. "Poor girl. But you know how Kevin is. Always working on a new business plan. Don't be too hard on him. I'm sure he'll show up soon."

Blowing her nose again, Alexis clutched DeeDee's arm. "DeeDee, this is terrible. I can't believe we're here because of Mother's death. I truly can't." She paused. "Maria, the housekeeper, said Mother was stumbling around when she came home Saturday night. Her words were slurred." Alexis's chin trembled. "Do you think someone tried to hurt her?"

"Your mother?" DeeDee shook her head. "Nonsense. Honey was beloved by everyone. I can't imagine that being the case. More than likely, she had some kind of medical problem that none of us knew about or recognized."

"I guess so."

"Come now. Regret is a harsh taskmaster. I know if there was anything within your power that you could have done to prevent your mother from leaving us, you would have done it. We all would have."

Alexis squared her shoulders. "Still, I think we ought to find out what happened. Mother was healthy last week. And now she's—"

DeeDee offered a sympathetic smile. "I know, sweetie. When I lost my husband, I felt exactly as you do now. Helpless, confused, wishing there was something I could do to fix it or some justice to be found." She beamed at Victor. "How lovely to see you again, Victor."

Victor offered a reluctant smile. "Same here, DeeDee. I'm always happy to see you, especially when you come bearing one of your marvelous pies."

DeeDee bobbed her head and scooped up the pie once more. "Come into the kitchen and I'll cut us all a slice."

Just like that, the tension in the room vanished. Luke shook his head. DeeDee was a miracle worker. *At least there was one even-keeled person in Honey's life.*

"Mr. Harris, would you like to join us?" DeeDee asked.

"I would love to, ma'am, but I'm afraid I must see to some details at work."

"Oh." Alexis sidled close and placed a hand on Luke's arm. "It was nice to meet you. I look forward to seeing you again, Mr. Harris."

Luke fought back a laugh. *Is she flirting? Why on earth?* "Have a good rest of your day, and again, I'm sorry about your mother."

"If you need anything, you know where to find me."

He nodded, but every moment in Alexis's company suddenly made him more and more uncomfortable. "I will talk to all of you soon."

As they offered their goodbyes, he walked quickly to the front door, letting it shut behind him.

Stepping onto the porch, surrounded by the sweet scent of flowers and chirping birds, Luke frowned. Something was off. Not only with Alexis and Victor, but with Honey's death as well. It appeared her demise might not be as simple as a medical complication.

He mulled over that thought. His gut told him something was wrong. He had to find out more.

Meagan

$\mathcal{M}$eagan rang the doorbell at Piper's two-story home on Mayhew Lane and waited, clutching her Bible to her chest. The last two days had passed quickly—even though she had moved book club back to Saturday this week. Most members preferred the Saturday slot for now, and so Saturday it would stay.

Meagan studied the cars lining the drive. Almost everyone from their small group at Trinity Christian Church had arrived for the midweek Bible study. Sunset painted the sky in shades of lavender and rose as twilight's sweet hush descended.

Heavy footfalls sounded on the other side of the door, and it swung open. Jim Watts grinned at her, his blue eyes reflecting the bit of sky untouched by sunset. "Hello, Meagan."

Meagan smiled. "How is Piper's better half?"

"Mean as ever and just as handsome." He chuckled. "I hope you brought some of your famous lemon cake."

She opened her hands and shrugged. "Sorry. I'm empty-handed tonight."

"That's a shame. I told Piper I wasn't sure I could let you in without it. But I suppose I'll forgive you. I know how it works. Book club members get all the treats first, and we're lucky if there are leftovers."

She laughed and stepped into the foyer. "You'll be happy to hear the book club is growing. We have a new member. A man."

Jim arched a brow. "That's a brave fellow."

"He might be here tonight, actually. He said he hoped to attend if work didn't keep him away."

"Good, good." Jim smiled and ushered her into the living room. "In the meantime, try to keep my wife out of trouble."

"That's a tall order."

Jim laughed.

Meagan had set her Bible on an end table when an arm slipped into hers. The citrusy scent of Piper's favorite perfume wrapped around her. "Hey, friend. Not wearing any of my gorgeous makeup samples, I see."

Meagan grinned. "I didn't know I needed to for Bible study."

Piper arched a brow. "Makeover model Meagan, remember?"

Meagan chuckled. "I'm not interested in any modeling—or any potential matchmaking. Hash Brown keeps me busy enough."

As if sensing a dog was being discussed, a howl sounded from the backyard. Piper winced. "Speaking of dogs, Ulysses is not happy to be outside tonight while all the excitement is inside."

"Poor guy. He would probably be fine."

Piper ran her fingers through her hair. "He wouldn't do more than lick the guests to death, but I know not everybody is a fan of dogs. Ulysses is a lot of dog." Piper's pet was a seven-year-old Newfoundland who could easily have been mistaken for a small bear.

"I'll head out back in a bit and give him some love."

"Always appreciated."

"Did you get everything you needed for your article?" Meagan asked.

"In spades. Thank you for your help." Piper lowered her voice and leaned in. "You remember the lip-plumping gloss I tried?"

"Yes."

"Well, they plumped up all right. To the size of a tomato."

Meagan gasped. "What happened?"

"I think I'm allergic to it." She felt her lips and grimaced. "It's been two days and they still feel weird."

Meagan eyed her friend's mouth. "The swelling must be down quite a bit from what it was. You look okay to me."

"Thanks. I kept ice on them all day Monday." Piper shook her head. "The things I do for a story."

"You're brave. No one can argue with that."

The noise level rose in the foyer as more people arrived. Meagan turned to see Luke among the newcomers. He shook hands with Jim, but before he could step into the living room, Meagan spied Candice Sligh edging close. She sighed, watching the woman—about her age—try to strike up a conversation. Everyone knew Candice wanted a boyfriend. *I think she tries too hard sometimes.*

"Look at that," Piper said. "Seems like Candice found a new prospect."

Meagan nodded.

A guest called Piper's name and she scurried away, leaving Meagan to continue observing the pair alone. Now by the living room's fireplace, Candice tossed her honey-colored hair over one shoulder as Luke finished a story. Every now and then his eyes would rove around the room and brighten when he saw Meagan, but eventually they would return to the woman before him. *Is he interested in her?* It wasn't any of her business, really. For all Meagan knew, they were the perfect match.

She moved to the kitchen for a glass of water, waving to Ulysses through one of the kitchen windows. The large brown Newfoundland whined to be let inside. *Sorry, boy.*

Piper reappeared as Meagan was taking a sip. "Good," she said. "I see he's settling down some." She blew Ulysses a kiss, then smiled. "Good boy. Come on, Meagan. Time to get started."

Meagan and Piper returned to the living room, a stylistic cross between farmhouse and classic Americana. The space was perfect for the fifteen or so people gathered tonight.

Meagan scanned the room for a seat. Her gaze landed on Luke, who grinned at her. She smiled back but moved to claim an empty dining room chair Jim had tugged out instead. Then she remembered—her Bible was on the other side of the room. *Lovely.*

Candice sat right beside the end table where Meagan's book lay, leaning in to chat with Luke on her other side. The blonde giggled and flashed her too-perfect white teeth. Meagan wrinkled her nose. Overt flirting wasn't her style. It would be better not to interrupt things. Meagan would muddle through the evening without her Bible.

Jim stood up and asked everyone to turn to Mark 4:22 and read it: "For there is nothing hidden that will not be disclosed, and nothing concealed that will not be brought to light." He surveyed the room. "What do you think this means?"

As others started to answer and a discussion began, Meagan's attention drifted to Candice and Luke. The woman leaned in close, whispering and pointing to the Bible. But Luke seemed barely interested. He'd nod, but his eyes remained focused on Jim. Before long, Candice took the hint and stopped talking. Meagan repressed a smile.

When the study time concluded, the room filled with familiar chatter. Piper rushed to Meagan's side and pushed her phone in front of Meagan's face.

"Check this out."

Meagan took the device, her eyes sweeping the social media newsfeed on the screen. "What am I supposed to see?"

"What Honey Northcutt's daughter is posting. I guess she has no privacy settings. Yes, I looked her up. Don't give me that face. I'm a journalist. Snooping is in my blood. Anyway, she thinks something isn't right about her mother's death."

"Hello, ladies." Luke's warm baritone sounded, startling Meagan so that she nearly dropped the phone.

She tried to recover her dignity with a bright tone. "I'm glad you were able to make it."

His expression dimmed slightly. "It's been quite a day. It was as though my phone never stopped ringing. All the more reason for Bible study."

Piper's eyes gleamed. "I'm glad you're here."

"What are you ladies up to?"

Piper smiled. "Long story short: we know Honey Northcutt is your client who passed away—sorry about that. I did some sleuthing after our comedy night. You looked so unsettled, I had to dig a little."

Luke frowned but didn't say anything.

Taking her phone back from Meagan, Piper held it out so the three of them could see. "See this? Honey's daughter is posting all about her. According to her, the housekeeper says the day Honey died, she came home from her card game stumbling around as if she'd been drinking."

"That's what Alexis said when I visited on Monday." Luke kept his voice low as he spoke, indicating they couldn't let this conversation go beyond their trio.

Piper shook her head. "Alexis also claims Honey was a teetotaler."

Luke crossed his arms. "What else is she saying?"

"She's demanding an autopsy. There's more, but it's hard to follow everything between her histrionics and the lack of punctuation." Piper tucked the phone into her back pocket.

"Not everyone can be as good at writing as you are, Piper," Meagan said.

Piper snorted. "Most people can end a sentence with a period, can't they?"

"I admit something felt off when I visited," Luke said. "But I'm glad Alexis is requesting an autopsy. I suspect that will delay funeral arrangements. To put it frankly, Honey's family is different. I don't feel completely comfortable with everything I've heard so far."

"Something about this whole thing has my journalistic instincts on high alert," Piper said.

Luke turned to Piper and said, "I can't ask you to help get to the bottom of this, especially since the family seems to be using official channels. However, if you and Meagan have time to investigate, I can't really stop you either."

Piper rubbed her hands together. "You know me—well, you don't, but I love playing detective."

"I'll help where and when I can," Meagan added.

"Perfect. If you were to work on this, here's what I'd recommend trying."

9

Luke

Thursday morning dawned bright, with white puffy clouds dotting a brilliant-blue sky. Luke tugged off his bicycle helmet as he parked his bike in front of his law office. He hoped the cheerful, sunny weather would bode well for today's mediation between Antonio and Stella. He swallowed the dry lump in his throat. He'd texted Antonio, asking him to meet today, but the man had yet to know the full reason for his visit.

Luke murmured a quick prayer for calm.

After opening the office and starting a pot of coffee, he relaxed in his leather chair, enjoying the steady *drip, drip, drip* of the percolating liquid in the corner.

A knock sounded and the door creaked open. Antonio's dark head peered around the corner. "Mr. Harris?"

Luke smiled and crossed the space to offer his hand in welcome. "Mr. Poppalardo. Please, take a seat. Would you like some coffee?"

"No thanks. I just came from Hammerheads Coffee Shop." He settled into the chair across from Luke's desk and patted his stomach. "I couldn't fit in another drop."

Luke poured himself a cup, then eased into the seat behind his desk again. "That's one place I haven't visited yet. What's your favorite item there?"

Antonio rubbed his jaw. "That's a tough call. Probably the cream cheese Danish. It melts in your mouth."

"I'll have to try that sometime this week." Luke picked up a stray pen resting by his notepad. "Do you know why I asked you here today, Mr. Poppalardo?"

The man arched a dark brow. "Please, call me Antonio. And let me guess, I'm here because I'm fascinating company? You want to pick the brain of a man crazy enough to try to tell jokes for a living?" He snapped his fingers. "Wait, I've got it. You want to break into comedy and need someone to show you the ropes."

Luke grinned and grabbed the comedy book from his desk drawer. "Unfortunately, no. Although this book is pretty interesting. I had no idea so much work went into creating even a small routine."

Antonio reached for the book and flipped through the pages. "I remember reading this when I was first learning the craft. Valuable insight here." He smiled as he thumbed through the volume, pausing here and there to read a line.

Time to be up-front. "Listen, Antonio," Luke said, catching his gaze. "The truth is, I'm a lawyer. Your mother-in-law's lawyer, in fact. She hired me to reconcile some disagreements you have—rather than sue."

"Sue?" Panic flashed in Antonio's eyes. "She can't be serious."

"Unfortunately, I think she is. However, I believe I can help both of you resolve this matter peacefully."

Antonio scowled. "Stella has never liked me, especially when she discovered I was a comedian."

Luke didn't reply, listening as the man talked through his thoughts.

"My wife, Missy, is great about it all. She has always encouraged me. I suppose we thought Stella would eventually accept it. Accept me."

Luke took a sip of coffee. "From what she tells me and what I've seen, I think Mrs. Jones's problem isn't that you're a comedian. It's your content. Why do you choose to include mother-in-law material in your act?"

"It's real. It's funny. Lots of folks have problems with their mother-in-law."

"Not everyone calls them out by name on a stage."

The comic grimaced. "Ah, come on, man. Details are what stick with people. And the mother-in-law bit is a gold standard. It's been around forever. It's universally loved because almost everyone can relate to it. Universal themes work." He blew out a breath. "What bothers me is that she went and hired a lawyer instead of talking to me directly."

"Sometimes it's easier to face perceived threats without having to show your face," Luke said. "I would say that your mother-in-law is opinionated, but not necessarily brave. Would you be willing to let me mediate your disagreement with her?"

"I guess. For all the good it will do."

Luke explained the process, then leaned back. "If it's all right with you, I will ask her to join us here in a few moments."

Antonio rubbed the side of his face. "I guess there's no time like the present, huh? All right."

"Remember, this is about reconciliation," Luke said in a soothing voice. "Building your family's future well-being."

Taking a breath, the man nodded slowly. "You're right. It will be okay."

Luke nodded. "The key is listening to each other. You don't have to necessarily agree, but find some common ground to build on. Try to see things from each other's point of view."

Moments later, another knock sounded. Luke went to open the door, pulling it wide to reveal Mrs. Stella Jones, who murmured a hello and took the remaining free seat across from the desk. She kept her head down, clearly avoiding eye contact with her son-in-law.

Luke settled across from them. "Antonio, Mrs. Jones, thank you both for meeting today."

Antonio frowned and crossed his arms.

Stella swallowed and fiddled with the sleeve of her flowery top.

"I know this is very difficult, but I believe that with time and communication, your family will greatly benefit from these meetings." Taking a notepad from his desk drawer, he clicked the pen and faced Stella. "Mrs. Jones, do you mind sharing why you came to me?"

Her bright-red nails were nearly wearing a hole through the sleeve of her shirt. "I need Antonio to stop making jokes about me in his act."

"Good." Luke smiled gently. "Now, I need you to look at Antonio and tell him that."

She faced her son-in-law, her eyes glistening slightly. "I need you to stop, Antonio."

The comic rolled his eyes. "Stella, that kind of joke is pretty standard."

Her chin lifted and her voice started to quake. "I don't like them."

Luke coaxed gently, "What don't you like about them?"

"Everything. They're mean." Her gaze dropped to her lap again and Antonio scratched an itch on his face.

"Do you know what I think, Stella?" The comic leaned forward. "I don't think the jokes are the issue. I think the problem is that you don't like me."

Her jaw dropped. "That's not true."

Antonio held out his hands. "What am I supposed to think? You told Missy I was wasting my time with the whole comedy thing."

Stella's eyes widened. "She told you that?"

"Of course she did. She's my wife."

The older woman stiffened. "Well, I wouldn't have said it if I thought she would say anything to you."

Luke put up a hand. "Let's focus on one thing at a time." He turned to Antonio. "Can you understand where your mother-in-law is coming from?"

"Not really. I mean, she never has been a big fan of humor.

Like the time we were all at the zoo. I made it my goal to get her to laugh that day and she didn't smile once."

Stella tensed. "You ruined the whole trip. Every time I took a breath, you were telling another dumb animal joke."

"I was trying to have fun, Stella. Those were harmless jokes and you were as sour as a lemon all day."

Luke took another sip of coffee. "What kinds of jokes?"

Antonio shrugged. "Silly stuff. 'What do you call an angry monkey? Furious George.'"

The woman's gaze narrowed.

Antonio continued, unfazed by his mother-in-law's ire. "Oh, and there was this one. 'What do you call an alligator with GPS? A navi-gator.' Or the one about why the animals won't play cards at the zoo—"

"Enough, please." Stella patted her flushed face. "Why can't you enjoy one day without trying to be funny?"

"I was trying to get you to laugh, Stella."

"You failed spectacularly."

"Let's refocus here," said Luke. "Antonio, surely you can see her point of view. You didn't care for her talking about you to Missy. Do you see how she might view your mother-in-law jokes the same way?"

"Yeah, I guess I could see how *she* would think that."

"What is that supposed to mean?" Stella demanded, her voice rising several pitches.

Antonio tapped his foot against the floor. "Come on. You know you don't have the greatest sense of humor."

"I can take a joke—just not the ones you tell about me."

Antonio shook his head. "You've got to learn to laugh at stuff like that."

She stiffened, the lines around her mouth deepening. "Everything is all fun and games to you, isn't it?"

"No, but I don't take myself so seriously that I can't function."

"Okay." Luke held up his hands. "You're dredging up old hurts, but you aren't empathizing with each other's perspectives."

Silence stretched taut in the room. Luke held his peace as the two of them glared each other down. A quote by Charles M. Blow skittered through his mind. *One doesn't have to operate with great malice to do great harm. The absence of empathy and understanding are sufficient.* He thought he really should hang that on the wall next to the other artwork. It might help with mediation sessions.

Stella huffed. "I don't even know why we're trying. This is ridiculous."

"*You're* ridiculous," Antonio replied. "You have never given me a chance."

"And why should I?" she retorted. "You use me in your jokes and expect it to endear you to me?"

"You disliked me before I ever set foot on a stage."

"It's a silly hobby."

"It is not. It's an art, and it helps people. My work is important to me."

Luke leaned into their line of sight. "This is a difficult and delicate issue," he said. "This situation has the potential to do harm to your entire family unit. Mrs. Jones, Missy is your daughter. Antonio, Missy is your wife. Both of you love her, right?"

"Yes," they chorused.

"Good. I would bet she doesn't like this situation either. No doubt it's stressful for her for the two most important people in her life not to get along. And she shouldn't have to choose between her husband and her mother. Both of you need to empathize with each other's viewpoints before we can move forward. Understanding how each of you interprets this situation is essential to resolving it peacefully."

"There's no understanding on Stella's part," Antonio snapped. "All she wants is to ruin my passion. She's disliked me since we first met."

Stella's face fell. "Why do you keep saying that? It's not true."

Her son-in-law's eyes flashed. "Then what's the problem?"

"You don't understand how deeply your act has embarrassed me. You drag our private family business—especially mine—into the open for others to ridicule."

"All comics do mother-in-law jokes."

"Your so-called jokes are affecting my personal life."

Antonio gaped at her. "What do you mean?"

Stella straightened in her chair. "A few weeks ago, I was eating at the Blue Water Grill with Roger, my husband. He'd gone to use the restroom, and while he was away, a couple approached me. It was a husband and wife who had seen Antonio's act."

"How did they know you and Antonio are related?" Luke asked.

Biting her lip, she looked down. "They suspected it because I was using a lint roller on my shirt."

Antonio chuckled, but cut off the sound with a cough.

Stella glared in his direction.

"I'm missing something," Luke said. "How would a lint roller connect the two of you?"

Stella's lip firmed into a hard line. "I use them often to keep my clothes neat throughout the day. It's a harmless little quirk. Apparently, Antonio made a bunch of jokes about it. That day, I was wearing a black top and noticed some cat hair on my shoulder, so I pulled out my lint roller to get rid of it. After all, who wants cat hair all over them while they eat? Anyway, the couple saw me, asked if my name was Stella—which I confirmed because I didn't know what was happening—and then they had the nerve to ask for a photo with me. They told me they wanted to post it on Antonio's fan page online. I was so mortified that when Roger got back, I demanded we leave the restaurant."

Antonio crossed his arms. "At least you didn't pull out the detergent pen you keep in your purse."

Her eyes narrowed. "Do you mention that in your little act too?"

"Sometimes." Antonio examined her. "Since when do you and Roger visit places like the Blue Water Grill? You're so cheap that if you died, you'd walk toward the light just so you could turn it off."

"How dare you!" The woman rose, fists clenched. "I demand that you stop talking about me. It's stop or be sued, you understand? Don't mention my name, my quirks, my habits—any of it. Stay out of my business."

Snatching her purse, Stella stomped out the door and let it slam shut behind her.

Antonio fell back against his cushioned chair with a groan. "That woman." He kneaded the back of his neck. "You're right, you know."

Luke tilted his head. "About what?"

"About not making the situation worse for Missy. We found out she's expecting."

The admission caught Luke off guard. "Wonderful news. I believe congratulations are in order."

"Thank you." The comic raked his hands through his dark hair. "I can't have her upset. And what kind of drama will my child be subjected to if he's living under the cloud of an unhappy father and grandmother?"

Luke paused. *Perhaps Antonio's baby is the key to ending this squabble.* "Indeed. Family dysfunction has a ripple effect. The words spoken and the deeds done now can change the next generation, whether for good or bad." He studied the man before him. "Does Stella know she's about to become a grandmother?"

"No," his voice rasped. "I have no idea how she'll respond."

"Mmm." Luke leaned back in his chair, the soft leather squeaking quietly. "There are bigger things at stake than personal preferences and pride."

"Yes, there are."

"I'll talk with your mother-in-law after she's cooled off. In the meantime, it might be good to consider new material for your act."

The comic grimaced. "That's like telling a Southern comic to lay off the redneck jokes."

"Do it for your wife and your baby, even if you can't do it for Stella."

Antonio crossed his arms. "I guess that's fair. I'll try to take it easy."

"Thank you."

Antonio thanked Luke for his time. Then the pair walked to the door and said their goodbyes.

Finally alone, Luke sat down and thought about what he'd just witnessed. Two people upset by circumstances and hesitant to reach a resolution amicably. One thing was certain. If he didn't make headway between the two, their family would suffer. *I can't allow that to happen.*

Stretching the tension from his muscles, he stood. A quick visit to the bookshop next door would clear his head. Maybe he'd even grab a book to help the situation.

Locking the front door behind him this time, he made his way to Rose Cottage Books and stepped inside. The aroma of paper, fudge, and brewing coffee wrapped around him like a hug. The tightness loosened in his shoulders. Nodding at two customers milling around the new-release section, he moved to history and smiled when he found Meagan standing before a row of biographies, a book in her hand as she searched the titles.

"Hey, Meagan."

She jumped and nearly dropped the book before turning to him with a smile. "You surprised me."

"Sorry about that. I scared you at Bible study last night too."

"Don't worry. I guess I'm too engrossed in my work sometimes."

"That's not a bad trait." He slid his gaze toward the volume in her hand. "Shelving some new arrivals?"

"Replacing a few popular ones that sold out." She held it out to him. "*The Life of Teddy Roosevelt* has sold quite well in the past month."

He took the book and flipped through the pages, eyeing the glossy black-and-white photos that popped up every now and then. "I haven't read it, but it looks great. I think I'll buy it."

Meagan grinned. "Music to my ears. How is your day so far?"

"Stressful."

"I'm so sorry."

"Comes with the territory." His phone rang in his pocket and he shot Meagan an apologetic smile as he accepted the call. "Hello?"

"Luke?"

"Yes."

"It's Piper. I thought you might like to know that Alexis posted on social media a while ago and said that the family has officially requested an autopsy on Honey."

"Good to hear."

"My thoughts exactly. Say, I was thinking. My brother's a detective in Boston, and he talks about exhausting all angles, checking out every possible lead. With that in mind, I believe a key to solving this mystery might be the housekeeper who noticed Honey's odd behavior on the evening of her death. Maybe we could have a short chat with her—informal, of course—to get her take on everything. What do you think?"

Luke considered it. He didn't know anything about the housekeeper beyond that her name was Maria, but knowing Piper's connections, he was sure she could find out more about the woman. "Yes, I believe that would be all right."

"Excellent. I'll see if I can dig up her details and text you later."

"Thank you. Bye."

He ended the call and smiled at Meagan. "That was Piper. She's a go-getter, isn't she?"

Meagan laughed, making her way up to the counter with him. "You have no idea."

10

Meagan

"Piper is certainly fired up."

Meagan chuckled at Avery's description of their friend. "What do you mean?"

Her friend's voice chirped merrily through the phone. "I was at one of my rental properties when she called, going on and on about the need to solve a mysterious case. She had all the energy of an Olympic sprinter."

"That sounds like Piper." Meagan settled into her cozy living room chair, her phone pressed to her ear. Friday morning had arrived with a bang. She'd already fielded multiple texts and a phone call—all before she'd even left home. As soon as she sat down, Hash Brown jumped on her lap and snuggled close.

"Yeah," Avery said. "She talked my ear off. She was talking so fast I had trouble following."

"She's pretty worked up about helping Luke with the case of Honey Northcutt." Piper and Meagan had filled Olivia and Avery in—with Luke's blessing. Amid all the chaos, one thing was certain: the members of the Rose Cottage Book Club could always be trusted. "You know Piper's journalist instincts. It's easier to pry a dog from a cut of meat than to tell her not to dig for something juicy."

Avery laughed. "Don't I know it. Has she told you the story about the time she was sure a clothing shop was running a secret side business?"

Meagan grinned, remembering Piper recounting the story to her on a visit to the bookshop not long ago. "Yes. She was right too.

The store even went out of business because of her exposé." She rubbed Hash Brown's ears. "Let's see what happens this time."

Avery snorted. "Sounds like a lot of work to me. But I hope she helps Luke find his answer soon."

Meagan sighed. "The case is eating Luke up too. Honey was allegedly acting strangely the night before she died, and that's bugging him. Piper's trying to talk to the housekeeper, who might have been the last person to see Honey alive."

"Why not talk to Olivia? She's a nurse practitioner. She may have some clue about Honey's behavior, especially if it was a medical problem."

"Good idea."

Heading to the kitchen, Meagan switched on the coffee maker. No better way to welcome a workday than with a warm drink. "By the way," she said, "have you recovered from your bad date over the weekend?"

"Yeah," she huffed. "That was definitely a painful experience. Can you imagine? Flirting with someone he'd just met the minute I left to wash my hands."

"I'm sorry, Avery. You deserve better."

"Thanks. But you know what they say. Mr. Perfect walks into your life when you least expect it."

"That's right. In the meantime, if you need something to occupy your thoughts, keep your ears open about the Honey Northcutt situation. Meeting lots of people in real estate and managing rental property has its advantages."

"You got it. Hey, speaking of, I think Honey's boyfriend, Kevin, spends a lot of time at Lincoln's Marina."

Luke hadn't mentioned Honey's boyfriend, but it wasn't impossible that she'd have one. "How do you know that?"

"I was on Lower Main yesterday and could hear someone talking loudly about Honey. He seemed pretty upset. Another man with him told him to stop, but he kept talking, saying how Honey never liked sailing with him or doing much of anything with him. Then I saw him openly flirt with a woman nearby. Later, I asked one of the patrons about him. He said Kevin Chambers dated Honey up until her death. In the short time since she's been gone, he has been sailing nearly every day and enjoying single life."

Meagan frowned. "I'll tell Luke. I'm sure he'd like to know."

A knock sounded on the door, and Hash Brown scampered toward it, howling a greeting. "I've got to go. Someone's here."

"Okay. I'm praying that everything goes well."

Meagan ended the call and moved to open the door. Piper stood on the other side, with Olivia next to her.

"Morning, Sunshine." Piper breezed in, her eyes bright.

"Good morning. What are you two doing here?"

Piper seemed not to have heard her. "Did you hear the news?"

Meagan shook her head and closed the door as her friends dropped their purses on the kitchen table. "What news?"

"More robberies last night. The Fabric House and Saucy."

"Oh no." Meagan groaned. "What is Vanessa saying?" Vanessa McGrath was the owner of The Fabric House, and Meagan couldn't stand the idea of the expert quilter's sunny personality being clouded by something like this. "One time when I stopped in, she told me Nantucket feels so safe, she never locks the front door."

Piper cleared her throat. "She is pretty upset. The thief, or thieves, didn't take any of her money or inventory. They tore up a bunch of her fabric, though."

Meagan poured coffee for all three of them. She didn't like this robbery business at all. "But why *those* businesses? I would think they would be the ones with the least amount of cash on hand. What kind of robber steals from a fabric shop?" She shook her head as she handed her guests their coffee.

Olivia bit her lip. "Maybe the guy isn't a very good thief."

"He's been good enough not to get caught." Meagan poured a generous splash of creamer into her drink, then pulled her tablet from a kitchen drawer and typed in the names of the businesses that had been hit. "I'm going to see if I can find a pattern. It can't be mere proximity."

"Yes, that's it," Piper said. "Channel your inner journalist, Meagan."

Olivia chuckled, then sipped her coffee. "Piper, I don't think anything makes you happier than pretending to be Nancy Drew—or encouraging others to do the same."

Piper grinned. "Hey, Nancy Drew knows her stuff."

"So why are you both here so early this morning?" Meagan asked.

"Olivia thought it would be nice to pray together," Piper explained. "With so much going on, I figure it can't hurt."

"That's thoughtful of you," Meagan said. "But before we get started, I have a question for you, Olivia."

"Shoot."

Meagan took a breath. "You're a nurse practitioner. What could cause someone to act as Honey did the night of her death?" She filled her in on the details Alexis had recounted on social media.

"Medically speaking? Any number of things." Olivia ticked off the possibilities on her fingers. "A stroke, a diabetic insulin crash, vertigo. Even something like atrial fibrillation could cause that kind of behavior. Hard to say without examining her or getting her blood tested."

"Hmm." Piper tapped her fingers on her coffee cup. "Maybe we'll know more after talking to Honey's housekeeper. After all, we've heard all our information from either Alexis or Luke. Secondhand information is never as good as going to the source."

"I agree," Meagan said. "And you already said Alexis tends to bend toward the dramatic." Hash Brown whined, and Meagan reached down to scratch his head with a grin. "Thank you. I know you're nothing like that, buddy."

Olivia glanced at her watch. "We better get praying or we'll make Meagan late for work."

"Mind if I lead?" Piper asked.

"Go for it," Meagan said.

All three women bowed their heads.

"Father, I ask You to give us a day of answers and peace," Piper said. "If it is Your will, please give Honey's mystery a quick resolution, and grant Luke wisdom and discernment as he navigates his cases. Bless Avery, Meagan, Olivia, and me in our work today. I ask You to keep us all safe, and please reveal what has been concealed."

Meagan and Olivia added their own prayers, and the three of them wrapped up in unison. "Amen."

"That was nice," Piper said when they were done. "Good idea, Olivia."

Olivia grinned, placing her coffee mug in the dishwasher. Then she slung the strap of her purse over her shoulder.

Piper followed suit. "I'm off to talk to Honey's housekeeper, Maria. She agreed to meet me at Hammerheads Coffee. I thought a relaxed setting would be best. Wish me luck."

"Good luck," Meagan said. "But how did you get her information so quickly?"

"Let's say she has a connection who loves to chat."

"Alexis?"

"You got it. I sent her a message on social media and told her I'm looking to hire someone to clean my house once a week. I'd seen her posts mentioning a housekeeper and wondered if she would send me her housekeeper's contact information. She was all too happy to share Maria's details. Wasn't that nice of her?"

Olivia shook her head. "You're incorrigible."

"I know. Isn't it great?" Piper frowned. "Oh no. I completely forgot to tell one person—Luke. Would one of you mind giving him a ring or text while I review my notes about the housekeeper?"

"I don't think I have his number," Olivia said.

"I can do it," Meagan volunteered. "I have to tell him something else anyway." She started to type a text on her phone that would relay Piper's plans, Olivia's advice, and Avery's information about Honey's boyfriend. Then, realizing how long the text would be, she deleted it. She'd call him once Olivia and Piper left.

"Thanks." Piper stood. "I'll let you know what the housekeeper says."

Olivia offered a smile. "Have fun."

Piper strode toward the door, then paused. A news story played on the TV Meagan had left on in the living room. "Hey, Meagan, isn't that the comic we saw the other night?"

Meagan squinted as a dark-haired man filled the screen, a microphone in his hand. He stood before a modest audience. Grabbing the remote, Meagan turned the volume up until his voice filled the room.

"My mother-in-law once fell down a wishing well. I had no idea those things worked so well."

Meagan groaned. "That's him all right, Piper."

The camera changed to a news anchor. "That was Antonio Poppalardo, a recent addition to Nantucket's Bad Punchline comedy club. His popularity continues to grow throughout the area."

The screen showed Antonio being interviewed at the club. He smiled at the reporter. "It's been a wild ride. I feel very blessed with these new opportunities."

"Any plans for a tour?" the reporter asked.

"Not yet, but I am in negotiations for a full-length TV special. Stay tuned."

"Isn't it wild to think that someone on our little island might have their own special?" Meagan asked.

"Yes, it is," Olivia said. "What kind of comedy does he perform? Political humor? Family issues? Observational?"

"The act we saw was mostly mother-in-law stuff," Piper said. "It was a little harsh, if you ask me."

"Can someone build an entire comedy career on mother-in-law jokes?"

Piper shrugged. "He's doing it. We should go back. Some of the other comedians were great. Do you think Kyle would like a night out eating fried pickles in the company of your amazing, intriguing friends?"

Olivia's eyes lit up. "He probably would. We do enjoy a comedy show every so often."

Piper opened the front door. "Think about it. I'm off."

"Happy sleuthing," Meagan said. "Think you can crack the case?"

Piper squared her shoulders. "Never underestimate a nosy middle-aged woman loaded with caffeine."

11

Luke

*L*uke panted, wiping the collar of his T-shirt against his forehead as he finished his jog. *Home at last.* A light breeze lifted his damp hair from his forehead, cooling him. He walked up the drive slowly, using the short distance to stretch his calves. Then his mind focused on his growling stomach. A smoothie would both fill him up and cool him down.

As he approached the front door, he spied a small basket of cookies waiting on the stoop. A turquoise envelope was tucked inside. Curious, he plucked the note from the basket.

Sorry I missed you. Sending you a pick-me-up after this week. Love, Mom.

Luke smiled. His mother always knew when he needed encouragement. Lifting the basket, he found that the cookies were oatmeal chocolate chip, one of his favorite flavors.

Whistling to himself in happiness, he pushed open the door and carried the goodies inside. Another bonus of moving to Nantucket was that his parents and brother lived in the area. He would call later to thank his mom for the cookies and see if his parents wanted to grab dinner sometime soon, maybe at One Atlantic.

He padded to the kitchen and flicked on the lights, bathing the warm wood accents in an amber glow. The phone in his pocket buzzed. Setting the basket on the kitchen island, he pulled out the device, another grin spreading over his face when he saw the caller. Meagan.

He connected the call and opened the fridge. "Hello?"

"Good morning." He found himself smiling at the sound of her voice.

"I don't want to bother you, especially if you're at work, but Piper needed me to give you a call. Do you have a moment?"

He pulled out a carton of almond milk and placed it next to the blender. "I'm not at work yet. What's up?"

"She wants to let you know she's meeting Honey's housekeeper at Hammerheads."

He nodded. "Okay."

"And, um . . ." She hesitated, as if searching for the right words. "I got the impression she wants to talk to her alone."

Luke frowned. "Why's that?"

"She didn't say as much to me, but thinking about it from Maria's perspective, it might be easier if Piper showed up without you there. A woman-to-woman chat may provide more information too."

He pondered that. She was right. The housekeeper would likely be more open with just Piper.

"Good point. I was thinking of heading over to the police station to see what I can dig up. I need to know if they are going to investigate Honey's death."

"Good idea. Speaking of that, Olivia gave me a few suggestions for what could have made Honey stumble around before she died." She told him the conditions.

Luke closed his eyes. "Lots to think about. Thank you, Meagan."

"No problem. And if you go to the police station, ask for Officer Taylor. Arthur Taylor."

"Officer Taylor?" Luke scanned the kitchen for a notepad and pencil. Pulling open the junk drawer, he found an old receipt and a pen and jotted the name down. "A friend of yours?"

"Kind of. He's come into the bookstore a few times. Nice guy. He's young, but smart and anxious to prove himself. I think he'll point you in the right direction."

Luke leaned over the counter, stretching his back. "No arguments from me."

"I almost forgot." Luke grinned at the energy in Meagan's voice. "While I was talking to Avery earlier, she mentioned something interesting. She said Honey's boyfriend, a guy named Kevin, spends time at Lincoln's Marina. According to folks around the marina, he's been there a lot lately—sailing and socializing with anyone who will listen."

Luke pushed away from the island and opened the fridge once again. He found the strawberries and pulled out the carton. "That doesn't sound like the behavior of a man mourning his girlfriend."

"Maybe he and Honey weren't that serious." She sounded like she didn't believe it.

"Maybe." He checked his watch. *Plenty of time to head to the police station and marina.* Today's workload was light. "Okay, while Piper meets with Maria, I'll head over to chat with Officer Taylor and then hit the marina. With any luck, I'll locate Honey's boyfriend."

"Good luck, Luke. By the way, Lincoln's Marina has two locations. Avery saw him at the one across from Lower Main."

"Thanks for the tip."

"Anytime."

"And what will you be doing?"

He heard rather than saw the smile in her voice. "Holding down the fort at Rose Cottage Books, of course. Besides, I have my own mystery to solve."

His brows lifted. "Really? Do tell."

"Not until I'm sure there's something worth discussing."

"Fair enough. Catch you later."

"Goodbye." She hung up.

Luke mulled over the conversation as he ran the blender. Alexis had mentioned something about Kevin on Monday. Had the man finally bothered to stop by and give Alexis his condolences? Maybe he had, but enjoying the single life so quickly after a loved one's death raised a red flag for Luke.

After downing a strawberry smoothie and grabbing a quick shower, he jumped into his black Ford Mustang and headed to the police station. One lone cruiser sat in the parking lot. *It must be a quiet day.* Or perhaps they were busy attending to more break-ins. The rash of criminal activity on the island dominated local news these days.

Walking through the doors, he smiled politely at the receptionist behind the desk through the glass partition that separated her from the waiting area. She was a young woman with bright-blue eyes and big blonde hair in a style he hadn't seen in decades. Her nameplate read *Judy Chapin.*

She raised her head and studied him. "Hello. Can I help you?"

"Yes. At least I hope you can. I'd like to chat with Officer Arthur Taylor."

"What is the reason for your visit?"

Luke cleared his throat. *How can I put this succinctly?* "I'm a lawyer, and a client of mine recently passed. I'm concerned about the circumstances surrounding her death. I was advised to gain the perspective of Officer Taylor."

The receptionist tilted her chin toward a steel door behind her. "He's back there. Third desk on the left. I'll buzz you through."

"Thank you." He headed through the door as she instructed.

Luke's nose tickled at the smell of musty papers and antiseptic as he wove his way between officers' workstations until he reached the one Judy had described. "Officer Taylor?"

The slim, blond-haired man startled, rattling the stash of papers he held. His wide brown eyes snapped to Luke. "Yes?"

Luke offered his hand. "Luke Harris. I'm a new attorney in town. My friend Meagan Poe referred me to you."

The young man squinted. "Meagan Poe?"

Luke hoped he was talking to the right officer. "She owns Rose Cottage Books."

"Oh yes. I stop in from time to time. I enjoy her collection of classics." He pushed his oversize glasses up his nose and motioned to Luke. "Please have a seat."

"I'm sure you must be busy," said Luke, sitting down on a hard plastic chair across from the man. "But I need your help."

"How so?"

"I recently changed a client's will. That client passed away soon after signing."

"That's unfortunate."

"Very." Luke decided to get to the point. "Especially now that there are some red flags surrounding her death."

The officer's brows furrowed, causing a line to appear between his eyes. "Like what?"

"The night she passed, she returned home from a card game with slurred speech and a fumbling gait. Her housekeeper witnessed it." Luke fixed the officer with a direct stare. "The woman's daughter has requested an autopsy."

"I see. Any other witnesses?"

"Not that I know of. I'm tracking down the details of my client's estate, which is why I need your help. Are you able to look into some of my client's associations? I mean, if it's not overstepping." Luke shook his head. "I don't have your resources, and Meagan praised your intellect."

The officer smiled. "That's nice of her. I can do that. Did you want to file a report?"

"Not yet. I don't want to make trouble if there isn't any, but something about this feels wrong. Honestly, you would be suspicious too if you'd met some of the woman's family."

The officer's smile dimmed, and he cleared his throat. "Unfortunately, my hands are tied unless you file an official report." He grabbed a clipboard with a stack of papers tucked under the clamp and slid it in front of Luke. "If you fill this out, I'll be able to check it out. Fair warning—if I turn up anything, we'll have to launch a formal investigation."

"I would expect nothing less."

Officer Taylor swiveled to face his computer. "When you're done with that, we'll go through everything you know about your client and her associations."

After his conversation with Officer Taylor, Luke slid back into his Mustang and rolled his neck from side to side. Thorough—that was the best way to describe the young officer's investigative technique. He admired that in the policeman and thought that he'd likely hear from him soon.

Now for the marina. He passed the *Dolphin Gazette* office, the chamber of commerce building, and the Whaling Museum before parking near the wharf. A breeze brushed his cheeks, the scent a mix of sea salt and grilled hamburgers. Crossing the road, he stepped inside the yacht club and blinked to accustom his eyes to the dim light.

The room was decorated with gleaming wood in mahogany tones. Leather chairs were tastefully arranged in small groups. A huge window overlooked the deep-blue ocean waters, and a massive pool table sat in the far corner. The aroma of grilled meat and peppers drifted through the air. Judging by the slight smoky haze, there was a kitchen on the other side of the closed doors.

A few customers glanced at him, but most ignored him. He ordered a ginger ale and took the time to peruse the people talking.

Retired guys, judging by their age and casual manner. A man watched a basketball game on the room's plasma-screen television.

Raucous laughter sounded from a hallway to the left. Luke followed the commotion to see a stocky man with graying hair and a slight paunch telling a story as a couple of others threw darts at a board. He wore a button-down print shirt and khakis, and a thin gold chain dangled around his neck.

"So I said, 'Eat it? I barely want to look at it.'"

A man standing to his right shook his head. "Kevin, that's hog swill and you know it."

Kevin? This could be the guy. Luke inched forward.

The man named Kevin grinned. "Maybe it is and maybe it isn't. Tell you what, you meet me for a round of golf tomorrow morning, and I'll tell you the truth of the matter."

The other man snorted. "You can't afford nine holes, much less a whole round. Got too many debts to pay off."

Rocking back on his heels, Kevin smirked. "Shows what you know. You'll be licking my boots when you realize how much money I've come into. Honey left me a whole heap. You'll see."

Honey? That has to be him. Luke joined the group. A few of them turned at his approach. He lifted the ginger ale in greeting. "Gentlemen, don't let me bother you. I'm here for some darts."

A lanky man with straw-colored hair offered his hand. "Peter Billings. Nice to meet you."

Luke shook his hand and smiled. "Luke Harris."

The others made introductions until only Kevin was left. He offered a lopsided smile, but his eyes—assessing and cool—were trained on Luke's face.

"Kevin Chambers, Esquire, at your service."

Luke clasped his hand, noticing the smooth skin of his fingers.

"Esquire? So you're a lawyer then?"

Kevin's smile faded. "Uh, no. That's just something I say."

Peter coughed into his hand. "Gonna have to up your game, Kevin."

Kevin scowled but quickly wiped the expression away, returning his attention to Luke. "New to the area? Haven't seen you around here before."

"Relatively new. I recently opened a law office downtown. You might have seen it. It's right next to Rose Cottage Books. You know the pink shop on Old Wharf Street?"

Kevin shook his head. "I don't read books."

"That's a shame."

Kevin sniffed. "I get all I need from television."

Peter thrust his chin in Luke's direction. "I don't mind a good crime story every now and then. What about you, Harris? You read?"

"Every day." Luke took a sip of his ginger ale. "I've loved books since I was a kid. The enjoyment still stands today."

Peter shifted his weight. "What type of law are you in? Divorce attorney? Criminal?"

"My specialty is in estate planning and family law. I'm also a licensed mediator."

"Nice." Peter crossed his arms, face thoughtful. "You know, I could use some legal advice, especially in regards to my business. You feel like gaining another client?"

Luke bobbed his head. "Perhaps. Let me give you my card and we can talk."

"Sounds good." Peter took Luke's business card. "I'll reach out one of these days."

"All right." Luke slid his wallet into his pocket, sensing Kevin's penetrating stare.

"Say, law is a lucrative profession." A third man smirked. "I'll remember your name too. Might need you to bail me out of trouble sometime."

Peter motioned toward Kevin. "Our friend Kevin here has had a time of it lately."

"Oh?" Luke asked, trying to keep his voice light. "What's been going on?"

"Ah, my girlfriend passed away." Kevin tugged at the collar of his shirt.

"I'm so sorry. Was it sudden?"

Kevin nodded. "Yes. Very sudden. Guess none of us really know when our time is up."

"Ain't that the truth?" Peter shook his head.

"How long were you together?" Luke asked.

Kevin shrugged. "A few years. Maybe a little more. Honey kept track of all that mushy stuff."

Peter nudged Kevin with his elbow. "Don't let him fool you. This guy was gaga over Honey. Talked about her all the time, even before she agreed to date him."

"Really?" Luke smiled. "What was it that attracted you to her?"

"Her personality." Kevin crossed his arms and rocked back on his heels. "She was always larger than life. Always the center of attention in every room she entered. I told a mutual friend about my admiration, and she set us up on a date."

Peter slapped Kevin on the back. "Honey's bank account didn't hurt either, did it?"

Kevin flushed. The tips of his ears went crimson. "It wasn't like that. Honey liked supporting my business ventures."

"And what business would that be?" Luke asked.

Kevin puffed out his chest. "I'm an entrepreneur. I'm constantly on the lookout for the newest and most cutting-edge start-ups."

Placing his now-empty glass on a nearby tray, Luke stuffed his hands in his pockets. "So you're successful, I take it?"

"I do okay."

Peter chortled. "Okay enough to sweet-talk the single ladies in town."

Luke held Kevin's gaze. The man squirmed.

"It's harmless flirting. Nothing more." Kevin's phone rang, and he turned away from the group to answer. "Hello?"

Even with his body angled and the chatter of the men around him, Luke could hear a woman's voice on the other end. Whoever the woman was, she did not sound happy. Kevin ended the call without responding to her and faced the group.

"Wrong number." His movements were jittery, and he refused to make eye contact, but he quickly smoothed his worried expression into an easygoing grin. "Speaking of business, I have some to attend to. Catch you later, fellas."

Luke watched him depart and narrowed his eyes. Something about the man had Luke on high alert. What did he know about Honey Northcutt's death?

Piper

Piper sat across from Honey's housekeeper at Hammerheads Coffee Shop and watched the woman twist her fingers in her lap. Her dark hair was fashioned into a messy bun, and her dark eyes shimmered with uncertainty.

Piper smiled to put the woman at ease. "Thank you so much for meeting with me today, Maria."

She nodded, but her face remained solemn. "You're interested in me cleaning your house?"

"Possibly. I'm basically gathering research about the cost, expectations—all that good stuff." She straightened. "Of course, much of it will depend on my husband's opinion too." Reaching across the table, she patted Maria's arm. "Don't worry. This isn't a job interview or anything as stressful as that. I simply want to know what your services are and what they cost."

Maria blew out a breath, and a tremulous smile curved her mouth. "I can talk about that. And thank you for the coffee and doughnut."

Piper waved her hand in dismissal. "Of course."

The woman took a sip. "It's good."

Piper leaned against the back of the chair and studied Maria. "Tell me, how long have you been cleaning houses?"

Maria raised her gaze toward the ceiling, as if counting the number inside her head. "Maybe nine, ten years now."

"That's a long time." Piper pinched off the corner of her scone and popped it into her mouth. "Do you enjoy it?"

"Yes—usually, that is." Maria smiled, but Piper noted it didn't quite reach her eyes. "I do not enjoy some aspects of it, like scrubbing out bathtubs." She made a face, and Piper chuckled. "But I have been blessed with good employers."

"That's important." Piper wrapped her hands around the cup of coffee steaming before her. "Tell me, about how many hours do you work, and what is the cost if I wanted to hire you or another helper part-time?"

"It depends. If you hire someone through an agency, the cost will be greater because the agency takes a percentage of the fee." She dropped a pastry crumb on her lap and murmured in Spanish as she cleaned it up. "I am my own boss, so I can be flexible and work with the family."

"Interesting. So, if I wanted to hire you to help clean my house maybe two to three hours a week, would you be available?"

Maria winced. "I'm not sure. I think maybe not." She swallowed, the muscles in her slender neck bobbing with the motion. "My last employer recently passed away." A sheen of moisture glassed her eyes. "Her daughter, Alexis, has asked me to stay for now. She thinks she will be moving in."

Is Alexis that certain of her inheritance? Piper reached for Maria's hand and squeezed. "I'm so sorry. Were you close to your last employer?"

Maria grabbed a napkin to blot under her eyes. "Yes, very close. Honey was more than my employer. She was my friend."

"That's such a shame. How long did you work for her?"

"Five years." Her words grew thick as she tried to hold back tears. "She was always so good to me."

Releasing her hand, Piper waited a moment, giving the grieving woman a chance to compose herself. "Do you mind telling me how she passed?"

"I don't know." Maria frowned. "I came in at ten that morning and did all the cleaning and a load of laundry that day. On weekends, I usually stay late and make her meals for the week. Honey came home around seven that night, but she was acting strangely."

Taking another sip of her coffee, Piper watched Maria with a sympathetic expression. "How so?"

Lines deepened on either side of the woman's mouth. "She walked like she had been drinking. But she didn't drink. Ever. Her words weren't right either. Her sentences all blurred together, like something was in her mouth while she talked. Her eyesight was great, especially for an older lady, but it was as if she couldn't see well. It was terrible."

"I can imagine." Piper mentally made note of the details. *I'll write them all down later.*

"I asked her if she wanted something to eat, but she shook her head," Maria continued. "Said she wasn't feeling well and wanted to go to sleep. I was afraid she had the flu, so I helped her get to her bedroom. Then I put her food in containers and left. When I came back, she—" Her voice broke off with a sob.

Piper didn't press the woman to say more, but she reached across the table to lay a hand on her arm.

When she had calmed down, Maria began again. "Her friend DeeDee dropped off Honey at the door that night. They loved card games and had been at one together that night. I never imagined she'd never play again."

Piper squeezed Maria's hand. "I'm so sorry. Do you think she had a medical problem?"

"Yes. And no. Like I said, I thought it was the flu, but now?" She looked up, her eyes reflecting an internal tumult. "Now, I'm not so sure."

"Why is that?"

With a glance over her shoulder to make sure she wasn't being overheard, Maria leaned forward and dropped her voice to a whisper. "A couple of days before she passed, I heard Honey arguing with her daughter."

Piper leaned forward as well. "What were they arguing about?"

"Hunter, Honey's son. He was released from prison not long ago. She was so excited. Wanted to give him money to restart his life." She shook her head, strands of her dark hair escaping from the clip at the back of her head. "Alexis was furious."

"Why?"

"She didn't think her mother should give him more money."

Piper started at that. "*More* money?"

Maria's gaze dropped to her lap. "She gave Hunter money once before. He used it to buy bad stuff. But that was before he went to jail. After, he changed, so Honey wanted to help him. But Alexis said she would 'fix things' if Honey gave Hunter the inheritance Alexis believed was hers."

That's a lead for sure. "I'm so sorry for all you're going through."

Maria offered a thin smile. "It's okay. Thank you for the food and coffee. I'm sorry I can't promise to come work for you. Maybe ask again in a few weeks. Alexis says Honey's lawyer thinks the court should have the inheritance settled by then, so I'll know whether I'm available based on whether she gets the house."

Chuckling, Piper waved her hand. "It's all right. I'm not sure my husband would agree anyway. Text me if you ever need to talk, or if your schedule changes."

Maria nodded. "You are very kind."

As they parted ways, Piper stepped outside and released a cleansing breath into the fresh air and sunshine. Pulling out her phone, she texted Meagan.

Got time for a short walk?

The reply appeared a minute later. *I think so. Hattie has arrived for her shift. I'll see if she can handle things for a bit.*

Smiling, Piper tapped out, *Okay.*

She says she's fine with that.

Piper started her Range Rover. *Pick you up in five.*

She then used talk-to-text to message Luke. *Had an interesting talk with Maria, Honey's housekeeper. Tell you more later.*

Piper pulled up to Rose Cottage Books and called Meagan to let her know she had arrived. She grabbed her sunglasses out of her purse and put them on while she waited.

The bookshop owner emerged from the shop, her smile bright as she climbed into the Range Rover and put on her seat belt.

"Brandpoint Beach or Chisler's?" Piper asked.

"Brandpoint. I love walking there." Meagan appraised her friend, eyes brimming with curiosity. "How did it go?"

Piper filled her in on the details of her conversation with Maria as she drove toward the beach.

"Well, what do you think?" Meagan asked when she was done.

"I think my mind feels like a spectator at a tennis match trying to sort through all of this." Piper pressed a button and the car's skylight opened, flooding the interior with sunshine and cool wind. The rush of air whipped their hair around their faces. Piper flashed Meagan a grin. "Next best thing to a convertible."

Within a few minutes, Piper steered into the parking area for Brandpoint Beach and shut off the engine. "I don't have to be at my computer until after lunch, so let's make the most of it."

She climbed out of the SUV and gazed at the lighthouse that stood like a sentinel on the edge of the beach. The white structure had been there since long before she was born, watching over the people of Nantucket for hundreds of years. She took comfort in its faithful presence.

Skirting alongside it, the women walked beyond the tall grass and strolled over the packed sand. Seagulls cried overhead, circling the water as they searched for fish. The breeze played with Piper's hair as the scent of ocean water filled her nostrils.

Stepping over a chunk of driftwood, Meagan asked, "Do you think Maria knows more than she's saying?"

Piper hesitated as she considered the possibility. "I don't think so, but who can say for sure? She seemed genuinely dismayed by Honey's death."

"That's so sad. I imagine it's rare for a housekeeper to have such a close relationship with her employer. Now, not only does Maria have to cope with her friend's death, but the future of her career is uncertain as well."

"Yes." Piper kicked at a broken seashell near her foot. "We need to know more." She growled. "It's days like this when I miss writing investigative pieces. In-depth profiles on the pros and cons of different mascaras don't quite scratch the frontlines-journalism itch."

Chuckling, Meagan stooped to pick up a shell. "I doubt many people end up doing what they originally pursued. Life has a way of slipping in plot twists at the most inopportune times."

Piper laughed. "Philosophical analysis from a true booklover. Plot twists, huh?"

"Sure. We're all characters living out our own stories. Each day is a page in our character arc."

Piper groaned and nudged Meagan's shoulder. "Stop."

Their amusement faded as they walked on. Piper revisited her conversation earlier that day. Was Maria as genuine as she seemed? And what would Luke think? Her focus shifted to the people around her. A couple picnicked on the sand. A grandmother held a toddler's hand as he edged close to the water, squealing as the surf lapped his toes. They all seemed so innocent, so pure. Untouched by the drama surfacing in their small town. A tinge of melancholy seeped through her heart.

"I hate the thought of a death from foul play on our sweet island," Meagan said, echoing Piper's thoughts.

"It *is* upsetting," Piper agreed. "But maybe Honey died of natural causes after all. Maybe we're paranoid."

Meagan shot her a sidelong glance. "So you're done investigating?"

"Absolutely not." Piper lifted her chin. "You were just talking about plot twists. You went from librarian to business owner. I'm going from reporter to detective."

Meagan raised a brow. "I'll let Officer Taylor know you're after his job."

Piper stopped to face Meagan. "Let's think through this. Maria notices Honey acting weird when she comes home from her card game. Honey goes to bed around eight. She passes away sometime in the night. No one else witnesses her behavior."

"Except for possibly the friend who drove her home."

"Right." She pursed her lips. "Alexis is furious that her mother might give her brother money and is planning on moving into her mother's house mere days after her death."

"Before the probate court officially announces Honey's last wishes." Meagan wrapped her arms around herself, though the day was warm. "Why would Alexis want to move in so soon? Does Honey have any pets that need tending?"

"Not that I know of." Piper studied the sand beneath her feet. Scattered seashells, pebbles worn smooth by the waves, chunks of driftwood—the remnants of the tide seemed as disjointed as she felt.

"And then there's the conversation Maria overheard about Hunter," she said. "I wonder—did he ask for money, or was that Honey's idea? Doesn't the state provide assistance for released prisoners?"

Meagan nodded. "Rosanne Reed—you know, the woman who runs the Celebrate Recovery ministry at church—has mentioned that the state has a reentry program. They help with housing, medical care continuation, employment, ID cards—a wealth of resources."

Piper scooped up a smooth stone and tossed it into the foamy waves, where it descended with a faint *plop*. "That's incredibly reasonable. Hunter should have all of his needs met."

"Maybe he wants more than his needs."

Piper grunted. "Who doesn't? Or maybe an indulgent mother can't stop spoiling her children, no matter how much it costs her." The wind tossed her short, wavy hair in every direction. "Do you really think Hunter is somehow involved with her death?"

"No idea, but it sounds like he and Alexis don't get along."

Laughter from farther down the beach drifted toward the women. It came from a middle-aged woman with red hair and a purple top walking beside a stocky man with graying, slicked-back hair. As the couple approached, Piper saw the woman smiling at the man. They appeared to enjoy the same sort of easy camaraderie she and Jim shared.

"Kevin Chambers, you're so funny."

Piper fumbled with her sunglasses and dropped them in the sand, drawing the laughing woman's attention.

"Oh brother," Piper muttered. "I knew I spent way too much money on those."

"Here you go." The woman stooped and retrieved the wayward glasses from the shore, knocking off sand granules as she handed them back. "They don't look too worse for wear."

"Thanks." Piper grinned and tucked them back on her head, secured by her thick hair again. "My picture is under 'clumsy' in the dictionary."

The woman laughed. "No harm done."

As the couple moved past, Piper bit the inside of her lip. "I don't believe it."

"Did she say Kevin Chambers?" Meagan asked, watching the pair closely.

"Yes." Piper turned to watch the couple follow along the shore, their figures growing smaller with each moment.

"That's Honey's boyfriend's name. Luke was going to try to track him down today," Meagan told her.

Piper raised an eyebrow after the retreating couple. "He and that lady are awfully friendly. Isn't it a bit soon for him? I mean, if it is the same guy. Honey only passed about a week ago. Shouldn't he be in mourning or something?"

"Maybe that lady is his sister," Meagan suggested. "Or a cousin. Or maybe—"

"Maybe we're jumping to conclusions," Piper finished.

They resumed their walk.

"You know Alexis Northcutt through social media," Meagan said. "What do you think of her?"

"The question of the century. I've read her posts and watched her behavior for a few days now."

"And?"

"I think she's trouble." Piper set her jaw, then added, "If I were calling the shots, I would say Alexis Northcutt is suspect number one."

13

Luke

Luke's gaze shifted between Antonio and Stella as they once again sat across from each other in his office on Friday afternoon. He felt like a schoolteacher trying to calm two quarreling students.

"Remember, both of your feelings are valid, but we must stay in the present, not live in the past."

Stella sighed. "I'm trying."

Antonio scowled. "Is that why you brought up the time you thought I'd stolen your TV remote?"

Stella tensed. "I knew exactly where it was until you and Missy showed up for a visit. Then all the sudden it disappears, and I'm supposed to think you had nothing to do with it?"

Antonio crossed his arms. "Why on earth would I steal your remote, Stella? There would be no point. It wouldn't work on my TV."

"It was a universal remote. Do you know how expensive those things are?"

Groaning, Antonio dropped his face into his hands.

Luke cleared his throat. "Stella, is it possible the remote may have simply been lost?"

She hesitated. "Sure. I guess anything is *possible*."

"Good." He smiled. "That's a start, however small. Again, you both keep fixating on the past. Let's focus on today. The issue we are dealing with is Stella being used in Antonio's stand-up routine." He turned to the comic. "Do you understand how this might upset her?

How it might upset anyone?"

Antonio bristled. "I guess. But I would think the attention would be flattering. Any attention is good, right?"

Stella shot him a withering stare. "Are you crazy? I—"

"Hold on a minute, please." Luke held up his hand and focused on Antonio. "That's interesting. Tell me, what were you like as a child?"

"I don't know." Antonio shrugged. "The class clown. I loved to prank other kids. Got my fair share of detention but was never in any serious trouble."

"Would you say you received a lot of attention from your parents?"

Antonio coughed. "I'm the middle of seven kids, so, no."

"Do you see what I'm getting at?" Luke asked. "Performing is a way for you to receive the attention you've always desired. You view any attention as good, so you personally wouldn't mind being teased in a crowd."

"Okay. I understand what you're saying."

"Good." Luke smiled. "The problem is, not everyone else feels that way. For some people, attention is embarrassing. It's like being singled out among peers."

Stella bobbed her head. "Yes, that's how I feel."

Luke released a tight breath. *Finally, we're getting somewhere.* "What's the solution here?"

Stella smiled shyly. "If Antonio agrees to stop doing the mother-in-law material, I will let bygones be bygones."

Antonio frowned. "That's not a solution. That's you getting your way. Do you realize how much of my act is made up of those jokes?"

Her eyes narrowed. "Almost all of it, from what I hear."

"I can't magically write new material in a day. People expect these jokes from me. It's part of my brand as a comedian." He shot a look to Luke. "I did try to write new stuff, but I can't come up with anything nearly as good as what I already have."

She glared at him. "Really? How hard is it to write a few new jokes?"

His eyes narrowed. "Do you realize how hard I work at this? It's a craft."

"Gluing popsicle sticks together is a craft that would make more money," Stella grumbled under her breath.

"I heard that." Antonio jumped to his feet, his expression tight. "It's impossible to reason with you, Stella."

Rising, Stella propped her hands on her hips and jutted her chin forward. "It's equally as impossible to reason with you, Bubbles the comedy clown."

Grabbing her purse, she stormed out the door with Antonio close behind, still arguing.

Once the door had slammed behind them, Luke tilted his head against the back of his chair, his gaze fixed on the ceiling.

Those two severely test my patience. But they will get there. I hope.

Luke grabbed his phone. He needed a break. He dialed Meagan's number.

"Hello?"

"Hey, Meagan. It's Luke. I need to clear my head for a bit. Do you want to get a late lunch with me at Hammerheads Coffee Shop?"

"That sounds great. Meet you over there in ten?"

"Perfect."

He hung up and rubbed his tight shoulders. Surely the day couldn't get any more eventful. Could it?

Luke waved to Meagan as she walked into Hammerheads Coffee Shop. She smiled and approached the nautically themed counter. Life preservers, fishing nets, and the shop's beloved cartoon shark mural decorated the walls, a sharp juxtaposition to the aroma of coffee hanging thick in the air. After ordering a chicken salad sandwich and tea, Meagan settled across from him at the small table he'd secured.

He sipped his coffee. "Thanks for meeting me. It's been a wild day."

Meagan smiled and picked up her sandwich. "I met Piper for a walk earlier, and she filled me in on what's going on. Sounds like she had a productive chat with Honey's housekeeper."

Looking around the restaurant, Luke lowered his voice and leaned in. "Yes, she told me the same. Meanwhile, I met with Kevin Chambers."

"Really? Did Piper tell you she thought we saw him at the beach earlier?"

Luke grimaced. "What a coincidence."

"How did your talk with him go?"

He drummed his fingers lightly against the table. "The man is trouble, in my opinion. He thinks he's a smooth talker, but he's oblivious to how he comes off to others."

"How so?"

"He spent a lot of the conversation attempting to puff himself up. According to the other men at the marina and Piper's report, he might be something of a Romeo-wannabe as well."

Meagan winced. "That's not good. Romeo died."

"True." Luke speared a pickle from his plate and chewed thoughtfully. "I heard him telling someone at the marina he was coming into some big money, but it may have been nothing more than trying to make himself look important."

"Maybe he has low self-esteem. The lower his confidence, the more he has to inflate himself to be accepted."

"That's possible."

Meagan stirred her tea. "What do you think?"

"I'm not sure," Luke admitted. "Something surprising happened right before he left, though. His phone rang, and when he answered, I heard a woman on the other end."

"What was she saying?"

"I couldn't tell. It sounded like Alexis, though. Surprisingly, I didn't have to wait long to confirm my suspicions. Alexis called me right before a meeting with my other client."

Meagan polished off her sandwich. "She did?"

"Yep. She said she didn't know who to talk to, but she thought I might be a good ear. I'm not sure why. I'm probably one person she shouldn't talk to, but she thinks otherwise. So I let her talk. She told me that Kevin wasn't who he appeared to be. When I pressed her about it, she confessed that she'd hired a private detective to investigate Kevin's past." He rubbed his chin thoughtfully. "It was a bit of a bombshell."

"What was?"

He lowered his voice to a whisper. "The detective discovered Kevin's real name isn't Kevin Chambers. It's Kevin York."

Meagan leaned forward, her face bright with interest, and Luke noticed she had golden flecks in her brown eyes. "So, Kevin has a different name and is bragging about coming into money." Her lips pressed into a thin line. "And Alexis is obviously leery of the guy. But is it because he's a creep or because he might stand in the way of her inheritance?"

"Good question. Seems to me they're both suspects. Both have a motive for wanting Honey out of their lives." Luke kneaded the back of his neck. "I'd like to talk to Victor Northcutt."

"Who is that?"

"Honey's brother-in-law. He holds a grudge against her and his brother."

Meagan gulped the rest of her tea and stood, her eyes sparkling. "No time like the present. Let me text Hattie about minding the store until I get back." She pulled out her phone, her fingers flying over the screen. "Okay, I got a thumbs-up from her. Let's go."

He tilted his head. "Just like that?"

"Might as well make hay while the sun shines."

Smiling, he rose and pushed in his chair before grabbing his to-go cup. "If we were detectives, I'd be Sherlock and you'd be Watson."

Meagan shot him a teasing grin over her shoulder as she walked toward the exit. "No way. I'm always Sherlock."

He laughed and followed her to his car. As he slid behind the wheel, his phone buzzed. Meagan's brow rose, and he shrugged before accepting the call. "Hello?"

Someone cleared his throat on the other end of the line. "Mr. Harris? This is Officer Arthur Taylor. Uh, do you have a few moments to chat?"

"I do, actually."

"Good. Meet at my office, please."

"Okay. I can be there in a few minutes." He glanced at Meagan, who studied him from her seat.

"Thanks." The officer hung up.

"What's going on?" Meagan asked.

Luke tapped his fingers on the steering wheel. "We have to make a detour to the police station."

"Let's go."

Judy ushered them through the precinct, and soon Officer Taylor's desk loomed ahead. Luke noticed the officer seemed much calmer, his expression serious. "Hello, Mr. Harris." The young man pushed his glasses up the bridge of his nose. "Sorry to take you from your work."

He held out a hand to shake. "And Miss Poe. Nice to see you again."

"Good to see you too, Officer Taylor."

Luke shifted to allow Meagan to sit first.

Officer Taylor held up a hand. "I'm sorry, Miss Poe, but I will have to ask you to wait back at reception, actually. This is between Mr. Harris and me."

Luke shook his head. "She can stay. She knows about my suspicions, and I trust her."

The officer sighed. "Very well." While Luke took the plastic chair beside her, Officer Taylor eased into his chair behind the modest office desk. He swiveled to reach for a file, flipped it open, and studied the page inside. "Per your request, Mr. Harris, I did a bit of investigating into Mrs. Northcutt's acquaintances and family connections. Most everything checks out fine."

Meagan raised her head. "Most?"

He handed the paper to Luke. "Look at the info for Victor Northcutt."

Luke scanned the report. "Wait. I don't see anything criminal here."

"There's not. But check this out." He tapped the page. "See his birth record?"

"Victor Northcutt is adopted? What does that have to do with anything?"

"Victor and his brother, George, inherited a substantial amount of money upon their father's death." The officer steepled his fingers. "But their father willed a much larger portion to George than he did to Victor."

"Playing favorites?" Luke guessed.

Meagan cringed. "What kind of a man would do that to his children?"

Officer Taylor shook his head. "Not a great father. It's not unheard of, though."

Luke set the file on the officer's desk as he puzzled out the news. "That's interesting. When I met Victor at Honey's home, he was angry. Said he hoped Honey had done right by her family—and him. He even mentioned how he loaned his brother a good sum of money and George never repaid him. He said something about making a deal with Honey too, now that I think of it."

Meagan scooted forward to peer at the report for herself. "Would he really hold a grudge that long? And why would George need money if he received such a large inheritance?"

Luke shook his head. "Good question."

"It's not really surprising." Officer Taylor leaned back in his office chair, and it squeaked. "George Northcutt went through a number of bad business ventures before finally finding success. All the old-timers in Nantucket know about it."

Luke murmured to himself. *Adoption, inheritance, old grievances.* "Is there enough here to open an investigation?"

"In and of itself, no. But that might change depending on the results of Mrs. Northcutt's autopsy. I will keep you posted."

"Thanks, Officer Taylor. You've been a huge help." Luke got to his feet, his thoughts tumbling. Now was there a possible link between Victor Northcutt and Honey's death?

He was beginning to feel as if the more they learned, the less they actually knew.

Meagan

Afer the visit to the police station, Luke dropped Meagan off at Rose Cottage Books rather than head to Victor Northcutt's together. Meagan had work to do and knew Hattie could man the store alone for only so long. Upon her return, Meagan took Hash Brown for a walk, then moved to her office to update the past month's transactions in her accounting software. She had just keyed in another line of data when Hattie entered. At her feet, Hash Brown wagged his stubby tail, happy to see his friend.

"Hey, Meagan," Hattie said. "Sorry to bother you, but I thought you might want to hear the news."

Meagan glanced up from her computer screen. "What's that?"

"Another robbery has been reported."

Now she had Meagan's full attention. "That's terrible. Where?"

"One Atlantic," Hattie said grimly.

"Oh dear. How much did they get?"

Hattie shook her head. "That's the weird thing. All of the money and electronics are safe. The thieves took a bunch of food and scattered a mess in their wake. There are pictures online."

Meagan did a search for *One Atlantic break-in*. A host of photos popped up along with a local news report of the incident. Meagan hummed in sympathy as she scrolled, taking in the damage—splintered crates with their contents scattered around the restaurant, broken glass jars littering the floor, smears of smashed fruit and bruised produce splattering the carpet near the front entrance.

She glanced back at Hattie. "This doesn't make any sense. Who breaks into an upscale restaurant only to scatter food everywhere?"

Hattie wrinkled her nose. "Beats me. It's similar to what happened at all the other places. Pure meanness on someone's part, I think."

"Perhaps." But Meagan wasn't convinced. She pulled her tablet from her purse and studied the notes she had hastily written that morning. Hattie was right. All the businesses had been ransacked, but not all of them dealt in food. *So what is it that links the robberies together?*

She added One Atlantic to the list. "Thanks for telling me, Hattie."

"No problem. Would you still like me to decorate the wall behind the Noah's Ark this afternoon?"

"If you get a chance. That would be wonderful."

"You got it." The older woman scooted out the door and Meagan returned to the list. If Luke and Piper could play detective, she could too.

Her phone buzzed, and she answered absently, her mind still on the robberies. "Hello?"

"Hey, Meagan. How's it going?" Piper asked.

"Okay. Just found out about One Atlantic. They were robbed too."

Piper groaned. "Not another one."

A soft knock drew her attention to the door. She smiled at the sight of Luke, who stood inside the office doorway, a pair of sunglasses in his hand. *I must have left them in his Mustang.* Meagan waved him in, and Hash Brown greeted his friend with plenty of demands for pets, which Luke happily supplied.

"Yeah, the store is a mess," she said. "How are you, Piper?"

"After our walk, I stopped at Saucy for a slice. They're recovering fine after their break-in, you'll be happy to know. But get this. A guy named Victor Northcutt is here with a friend." She dropped her voice, and Meagan strained to hear. "He's in the corner carrying on about Honey's estate. Any relation?"

Meagan's pulse tripped. "Really? That's Honey's brother-in-law. Luke mentioned him when we met earlier. Is he saying anything else?"

"Hold on." A rustling sound crackled the line before Piper's soft tone drifted through the phone again. "Okay, he says it's a travesty his brother ever willed his fortune to her and thinks since Honey is dead, the money should go to him."

"Yikes."

"My thoughts exactly. Listen, I have to go. He's going to notice me if I keep watching him and talking into my phone."

"Okay. Thanks for the information." Meagan hung up and turned to Luke, who was rubbing Hash Brown's belly. "Did I leave my sunglasses behind?"

He smiled, straightening and handing them to her. "Yes. I noticed them when I was getting something out of the car. Fortunately, your office isn't too far from mine."

"Thank you for bringing them back."

He nodded, his eyes sliding toward the phone. "Piper saw Victor?"

She relayed what Piper had said, and his expression darkened slightly. "What are you thinking?" she asked. "Did you go see him yet?"

"Not yet." He pinched the bridge of his nose. "I need to walk. To think. I know we've seen a lot of each other today, but do you want to come?"

She glanced at the time on her phone. "I can manage a few minutes. Hash Brown can stay here, though. He already had a walk."

After checking in with Hattie, the two made their way out the front door, leaving a drowsy Hash Brown behind. Seagulls wheeled overhead as they meandered down Old Wharf Street. They passed the wharf, watching two kids squeal as they tossed birdseed to the diving seagulls on the pier. Their mother sat on a nearby bench, laughing at their antics. The seagulls dipped and dived in circles, eager to retrieve the food.

"I've been thinking through everything," Luke began, "and I'm convinced Kevin Chambers is lying. Possibly Alexis too. And of course, Victor is one to watch."

She studied his strong profile. "Why do you say that?"

"I've taken some interesting classes while preparing to be a mediator. One of them covered how to spot deception." He chuckled. "Imagine my surprise when I learned there were FBI agents taking the same course alongside me."

"Wow." Meagan smiled.

"What shocked me the most is that there is no universal sign for lying. It varies from person to person and culture to culture. But patterns, gestures, and words can help give it away."

Her brows lifted. "What types of things do you see in Kevin and Alexis?"

He kicked at a pebble. "Body language, bumps in speech patterns, things like that."

"What does that mean?"

"Liars usually want to distance themselves from what they've done. They'll change an 'I' statement to 'it' or 'they.' Rarely do they use a first-person reference if they are lying and guilty. They'll also intentionally 'forget' specific details. Convenient amnesia is what I call it. 'I don't remember doing that.' You know, things of that nature."

"Fascinating." She brushed a wind-blown strand of hair from her eyes. "If you saw a transcript of a testimony, would you be able to tell if that person is lying based on the—what did you call it? Language bumps?"

"It's possible. Some people lie in other ways than word choice. Refusing to make eye contact or making too much eye contact is common."

Meagan scoffed in frustration. "How are you supposed to tell when they're lying if deception is part of both extremes?"

He smiled. "It's when a person breaks their regular pattern of communicating that you'll notice their deception. If they always maintain eye contact and then suddenly look away, something is going on. If they are usually direct and then become ambiguous, that's a sign." He stopped walking and turned to face her. "Let's test it. Tell me a lie."

Meagan shielded her eyes from the bright sunlight beaming down. "Tell you a lie?" She paused to think. "Okay, I'm going to tell you several things and we'll see if you can pick out the lie."

He narrowed his eyes at her, but his grin spread wide. "Do your best."

"Okay." She took a deep breath. "Piper has written stories for the *Chicago Daily* and the *St. Louis Chronicle*, but she's most recently worked for *Boston News Today*. I have a master's degree in library science. My grandpa Lincoln and grandma Nell started the marina in Nantucket." She fought back a laugh at his studious expression. "My favorite ice cream is chocolate, and Avery has a ten-year-old cat named Beatrix." She smirked. "Pick the lie."

"Hmm." He rubbed his jaw and then grinned. "The lie is your ice cream flavor. Chocolate is not your favorite."

"How do you know that?"

"You gave very specific information in the other three. That one was too generic."

"Got it on the first try. For the record, my actual favorite is mint chocolate chip." She grinned. "Tell me a lie now."

Meagan's breath caught in her chest as he held her gaze. *He's even more handsome up close.*

"My brother's name is Tim. I love doing any kind of outdoor sport. My favorite research involves the Constitution and historic court cases. I love my dog Samson." Her pulse beat faster as he leaned closer. "And you have a very nice smile."

Meagan's heartbeat raced as she processed his words. "Was that—" Her voice cracked, and she swallowed and tried again. "Was that last comment a lie or the truth?"

He grinned. "Guess that's for you to figure out." He winked. "But if it helps, I don't have a dog named Samson."

Luke

Luke rubbed his eyes and pushed away from his desk. The weekend had rushed by in a blur. Saturday he had spent cleaning the house, going for a run on the beach, and watching a documentary on the life of George Washington, followed by another visit to book club. This week's meeting didn't contain as much literary discussion as last week, but fun was still had by all—except Piper, who had to miss due to deadlines. The other book club members spent little time focusing on the events of the week, all grateful for a comfortable moment among friends for a change. Sunday he'd worshiped at Trinity Christian Church and now, Monday was hitting with a vengeance.

He'd spent part of the morning on the phone with the probate court discussing the procedures for closing Honey's estate. The hours slipped past as he sent them copies of Honey's assets: real estate, stocks, bonds, jewelry—the list was endless. The final hearing was set for the middle of June, nearly six weeks after her death. Now, he had to contact all her beneficiaries to let them know. He winced, thinking of how angry Victor Northcutt would be when he learned he had been left out of her will. At least the autopsy would be concluded soon, and then her family could plan the funeral. All of them needed closure.

The door opened, startling Luke from his thoughts. He rose as Antonio Poppalardo marched in.

"Hello, Antonio. What can I do for you?"

The comic stopped at his desk, the lines on his forehead creasing and giving him a haggard look. "I don't know what to do, Mr. Harris. I've thought a lot about what you said, and I decided to reach out and call Stella. But she won't answer."

Luke examined the man before him. He had clearly turned a corner since their last meeting. Maybe his wife had talked some sense into him, for the sake of their unborn child. "I'm sorry. She's likely still wading through a lot of hurt. Don't give up."

Antonio slumped into the chair across from his desk. "Things are strained right now between my wife and Stella, but Missy, bless her, is trying to keep the lines of communication open. I didn't realize that what I was doing was affecting my wife's relationship with her mother. I never meant for that to happen." He sighed. "Missy called her yesterday, but Stella was too busy getting her nails done to talk." He shook his head. "The woman is typically frugal to a fault. And suddenly she's going to the nail salon, buying clothes and jewelry. It's totally out of character for her."

Luke puzzled over the change. "I wonder . . ."

"What?"

"Maybe she's trying to compensate for the feelings she's dealing with. You know, she's embarrassed by the jokes, so instead of hiding—which is the usual response—she's going out of her way to make herself feel better. New clothes. New nails." He searched Antonio's face. "What does your father-in-law say?"

Antonio lifted a shoulder in a half-hearted shrug. "I called him. He said the same thing you did. He told me when she's stressed out, she puts all her energy into shopping trips and gussying up. It helps improve her mood."

"This situation must really upset her."

Antonio slouched in his chair. "Guess so."

Luke laced his fingers together. "I spent a lot of time this past weekend pondering the best way to mend this rift between the two of you. For now, don't try to call her. I'll talk to her and contact you for another meeting."

"Thanks, man," Antonio said. "You've been great through this whole ordeal. I know Stella approached you first, but I want to be completely honest about the situation. Missy needs me to do whatever I can to fix this." He sniffed, his eyes glassy. "She's worth it. Our baby is worth it. My family is more important than whatever bit of fame I could build at its expense."

"Absolutely. I appreciate you talking with me. And with that attitude, we can definitely keep your family happy and healthy."

They shook hands, and Antonio left. The door had barely closed when Luke's phone vibrated in his pocket. He answered it.

"Hello, Mr. Harris? It's Alexis." The woman's nasal tone drifted across the line. "I've heard from the coroner's office." Her voice quaked.

His pulse jumped. "I see. Is something wrong?"

"Something called ethylene glycol was found in my mother's blood. I'd never heard of it before," Alexis said. "It sounds bad, though. Right?"

It sounded quite serious, but Luke didn't want to alarm her even more. "I think a lot of chemicals can sound bad, but that doesn't necessarily mean they are."

Alexis heaved a sharp breath. "What does it mean? What do I do?"

"I'm not sure, but I can find out. Can you email me the autopsy report?"

"Yes. What's your email address?" Luke gave it to her, and she sniffled. "Thank you for all of your help."

"Of course. I'll call as soon as I know more." He ended the call, thoughts whirling. Within moments, his computer dinged with an incoming email. He opened it with a click and printed it out.

Snagging the paper, Luke scanned the contents, a cold stone of dread sinking into his stomach.

He needed to call Piper immediately.

"What do you make of this?"

Luke tossed the autopsy report on the table inside The Lobster Trap, where Piper had agreed to meet him for lunch.

She took a bite of her crab cake sandwich and skimmed the report. "Wow."

Luke pulled out his chair but declined to order when the waitress approached. He wasn't hungry with everything that was on his mind.

Piper pushed away her plate and flipped the page. "Ethylene glycol. Interesting."

"Why is that?"

"I did a story about it once," Piper explained. "Ethylene glycol has no odor and tastes sweet. It could be the reason for Honey's slurred speech and strange behavior the night she died." She pointed to a line on the report. "The examiner found high levels of albumin."

"What does that mean?"

Piper narrowed her eyes. "She had liver failure. If I remember my old research correctly, ingesting ethylene glycol can cause the liver to fail like that. I think she was poisoned."

"Poisoned?"

Piper nodded. "If it was in the air, Alexis or Maria or someone around her would likely have been affected too."

Luke rubbed his hand over his chin as he sorted through the revelation. "Would Honey have ingested it on purpose? Such a thing would be—"

"A somber possibility," Piper finished for him.

Was that why Honey had come to him to change her will? Had the entire event been part of a premeditated design to leave her affairs in someone else's hands? Something didn't ring true about that scenario.

"Honey didn't seem troubled at all. In fact, she was excited that her children were turning their lives around, and especially that Hunter had just been released from prison."

"Maria told me the same," said Piper. "Could Hunter have had a hand in this?"

Luke shook his head. "I don't think so."

Piper tapped the autopsy report. "If Honey was killed, the person would have had to slip her the poison somehow."

"Does ethylene glycol process quickly?" Luke asked.

"I'm sure it does, but I'll do some more investigating to be sure."

"Yes, please." Luke crossed his arms. "Seems like someone would know if they were poisoned by a chemical."

Piper shook her head. "Not this one. Like I said, it has no smell and tastes sweet. In fact, that's the whole reason I wrote the article about it in the first place. A few years ago, a woman in Atlanta killed her husband with ethylene glycol–laced gelatin. It was a big story. And here." She pulled out her phone and typed before showing him the screen. "A man in Arizona poisoned his wife by mixing it into a cocktail of vodka, orange juice, and soda."

A sick feeling hit Luke. "So there's no other way for a compound to get into her bloodstream?"

Piper held up her hands. "Questions of that nature are for medical experts. All I know is that it's been used to kill people before."

Luke swallowed, his mind spinning.

"You know what this means, don't you, Luke?"

"I sure do," Luke said seriously. "It means we have a murderer in Nantucket."

Meagan

$\mathcal{M}$eagan pushed a noisy cart through Island Market, scanning the rows of dog food. Hash Brown had taken a sudden disinterest in his normal fare, and now Meagan joked that he likely wouldn't be happy until she served him prime rib on a platter. He was spoiled rotten, but she had no one to blame for that but herself. She grabbed a different brand of kibble for him to try and added it to the growing pile in the bottom of the cart.

Next she moved to the dairy aisle and noted the daily special—buy three, get one free on yogurt. She pulled four containers of Greek yogurt out of the refrigerated case and set them in the cart.

"I told you I wanted chicken, not roast beef."

Meagan turned at the sound of the voice booming at the deli counter. A red-faced man scowled at a female worker, who glared at him from beneath the line of her hairnet.

"Now see here, Victor Northcutt, you're one of my regulars and I appreciate your business, but I'm not going to let you bite my head off."

Victor Northcutt? Meagan pushed the cart closer.

The tall, wiry man glowered. "Come on, Betty. I'm having a hard time lately."

"That doesn't give you the right to bark at everyone in your path."

He crossed his arms. "Just give me my chicken, will you?"

With a huff, the woman briskly operated the meat slicer, weighed and wrapped the meat, and tossed it on the counter. "Here you go."

Snatching it up, the man headed off, grumbling as he went.

Meagan bit her lip and approached the counter. "I'm sorry he spoke to you that way."

"Don't worry about it. Victor has always been like that. I've known him since high school. Never has been the happy sort—less so after his brother died, and now Honey." She dropped her voice to a low whisper. "If you ask me, he's lonely."

If they talk to you, they will also talk about you. Nell's advice on gossiping drifted through Meagan's mind, but she whisked it away. This wasn't gossip for gossip's sake. She was trying to help Piper and Luke. "Who was his brother?"

"George Northcutt, God rest his soul. He was one of those fellows who liked to brag that he had a Midas touch, especially after he became successful. Ate Victor up something fierce."

"That's so sad."

"Can't fix the world's problems." She shrugged, eyes brightening. "What'll you have, sweetie?"

Meagan peeked into the display case. "Half a pound of turkey, please."

"Thin, medium, thick?"

"Medium slices." As Betty pulled the turkey from the case, Meagan pondered her words. "What do you think makes some folks celebrate another's success while others resent it?"

Betty pinched her lips. "Who's to say? I imagine parenting has quite a bit to do with it, but personality and disposition likely play a part as well. I would say most of it comes from an ungrateful heart."

"True." She drummed her nails against the cart. "Did Victor ever seem thankful for his brother or his own blessings?"

"Rarely." Betty placed the turkey in the slicer and slid it over the blade. Clean slices fell onto a metal scale covered with butcher paper.

"The man was especially bitter over George's marriage to Honey. Victor always had a hankering after Honey, but the woman wouldn't give him the time of day."

Meagan's ears perked with that bit of news. "Victor had a crush on Honey Northcutt?"

"Heavens, yes. He was positively silly over her in school. Told everyone she would be the one he married someday." She shook her head. "That all changed when his brother asked her to prom instead. Never did see two people fall in love so quickly."

Meagan filed that information away and promised to tell Luke and Piper about this discovery.

Betty finished her order and handed her the wrapped package with a smile. "There you go, my dear. Enjoy your day."

"Thank you."

Meagan meandered through the aisles, reflecting on the new information. Was Victor Northcutt merely a perpetually cranky man, or was it long-held bitterness that skewed his view of the world?

She added grapes, strawberries, and lettuce to her cart before checking out. Back at home, she put the groceries away and let Hash Brown out for some exercise, enjoying watching him try to catch birds and insects—even his own shadow. It wasn't until they returned to the carriage house that she glanced at her watch.

"Four o'clock already. Come on, Hash Brown. Time to drop in at the bookstore."

They drove the short distance to Rose Cottage Books. As Meagan pulled into a parking spot, she eyed the front of Luke's law firm—no car and no bicycle outside. *Is he at a meeting?*

It wasn't her business. She went inside her store, offering a smile to the patrons who moved through the rows of books.

After greeting some of the regular shoppers, she released Hash

Brown to play with his toys tucked in the back corner. She waved to Hattie, who was dusting near the register.

"Everything going okay this afternoon?" Meagan asked.

"Right as rain. Monday is always a good sales day here."

"Wonderful. I need to work in the office for a bit, but if you need to go home, feel free. You've helped me a lot lately."

Hattie waved her hand in dismissal. "I don't have anything pressing to do, and you know I love being here. I can at least finish the dusting."

"Thank you." Meagan moved to her office and set her purse on the desk.

A few minutes into her inventory spreadsheet updates, a loud crash sounded through the wall. Meagan gasped and jumped up from her chair. Had Hattie fallen?

She raced out of her office to see Hattie standing on a small stool in front of the nonfiction section, duster in hand. Hash Brown growled lightly at her heels, his gaze focused near the back of the building.

"What was that?" Meagan asked.

Hattie shook her head. "I don't know, but Hash Brown keeps looking outside, so let's start there."

Meagan bit her lip and glanced at the dog. His legs danced, and his ears stood at alert. She decided to peer through the window at the back of the store. If an intruder skulked in the alley, it was better to try to see him before he saw her. As she approached, a sigh of relief escaped her. Their two large trash cans were knocked over, bags spilling onto the alley.

"It's the trash." Meagan moved to the back door. She patted Hash Brown. "Don't worry, buddy. I'll get it cleaned up."

She stepped outside, ignoring Hash Brown's whines to join her. No wind moved. No one waited in the shadows. But as she went to pull the first can upright, something darted out from inside, blurring past her feet in a streak of brown and black.

She shrieked and fell back in surprise, landing with a painful thump. Hash Brown's barking echoed her fear. She thought about getting him but dismissed it. *I can handle this myself.*

What was in the trash can, though? A cat? A rat? She shivered. *No, that creature was far too big to be a rat.*

Slowly, she rose on shaky legs and approached the second fallen trash can with caution, her nerves on end. Her foot nudged the metal bin. A hiss erupted, echoing inside the small space.

Stepping close, she leaned down and peered into the can. Two bright, golden eyes blinked back at her before the creature burst out of the large container and scampered away.

She clapped her hands over her mouth, unable to believe her eyes. In the window, Hattie tried to contain a yipping Hash Brown.

"A raccoon. Two raccoons, to be precise," Meagan told them.

Shaking off her fear, she stood and checked the cans for any more invaders before propping them up once more. Trash collection wasn't until Thursday.

Let's hope we don't have more visits from the furry bandits before then.

Luke

Luke squirmed inside his Mustang. He usually enjoyed a leisurely drive, but this afternoon he was anxious. Anxious to talk to Hunter Northcutt. Anxious to be done with the whole affair.

The bright sunshine of the Nantucket morning had given way to pewter clouds. Raindrops pelted the windshield. The wipers squeaked with every swipe of the drizzle coming down. He passed a gas station and an antiques store before turning onto a narrow winding road. Squat older houses—many in need of a fresh coat of paint—flew by. Near the end of the road, his GPS announced, "Your destination is on the right." He steered onto the gravel drive, and a small white house appeared, nestled among the trees. A worn pickup sat outside.

Luke put his car in park and double-checked the number on the front of the house. *This is it.* When he'd called Hunter for a meeting, the man had been thorough in his instructions.

He climbed out from behind the wheel and approached Hunter's residence. A porch swing squeaked in the breeze, and by the look of them, some of the boards needed replacing, but overall, the spot was homey. Rain pelted Luke's face and arms as he skirted mud puddles forming in the yard.

Climbing the sagging porch steps, Luke knocked and waited. After a long moment, the door creaked and a tall man with sandy hair and a shy smile opened the door. He wore faded jeans and a gray T-shirt.

"May I help you?" the man asked.

"Hi. I'm Luke Harris. Is Hunter Northcutt here?"

"Hi. I'm Hunter." The man extended his hand, and Luke shook it firmly. "You found the place okay, I assume?"

"No problem." Luke released his hand with a smile. "Nice little house you've got here."

Hunter's eyes flooded with sadness. "One of my parents' small rental properties. My mother was kind enough to let me stay here after my release. Please, come in."

He ushered Luke inside to a living room filled with a worn sofa, tattered rocking chair, and small flat-screen television. Settling onto the couch, Luke regarded the man before him. Hunter appeared near his own age—around forty. His stance was curious but guarded. He could only imagine the details of Hunter's past, but the memory of Honey's love for him and her genuine joy in his release stood tall in Luke's mind.

"Thanks for your willingness to come here, Mr. Harris. Getting back on my feet will take a while. It's nice to be able to save a few bucks on gas."

"Feel free to call me Luke." He paused, wondering about the best way to proceed. "Have you heard from your sister recently?"

"Not much since the day I moved in here." Hunter swallowed. "I last saw her in person a few days before my mother's death."

"Such a loss must have been very difficult for you."

"Extremely." Tears glistened in Hunter's eyes, and he stared out the living room window. After a moment, he cleared his throat and asked, "Why did you want to meet with me?"

"Hunter, I need to tell you something. Your mother asked me to change her will a few days before she died. She decided to write you into it."

Hunter gaped at him. "She did?"

Luke nodded, handing him a piece of paper from the probate court. "I'm making my rounds delivering the news of inheritance to you and the rest of your mother's beneficiaries. But the exact details won't be released until the court hearing."

"I understand."

"And that's not all."

"I heard Alexis requested an autopsy," Hunter said, following Luke's train of thought. "She plastered it all over her social media account. But I don't know the result. Do you?"

Luke said he did. "Alexis told me."

Hunter went quiet. After a time, he spoke again. "They found something?"

"Ethylene glycol."

Confusion flickered across the man's face. "What does that mean?"

"It's a substance that can be deadly if ingested."

"My mother didn't do things like that."

"I don't think she did."

"Then what—?" As realization dawned, Hunter expelled a harsh breath and fell against the back of his chair. "No way. I can't believe it." His mouth was slack as he searched Luke's face. "But how? Why?"

"No one knows yet. The police should be talking to you soon, I imagine."

"Me?" He ran his fingers through his hair and shook his head. "What could I possibly know?"

"You were her son. You knew her better than a lot of people, I assume. The police will want to hear all about her. From the short time I knew your mother, she seemed extremely likable. Her friends and acquaintances have spoken very highly of her. The police will probably want to corroborate that image with as many people as possible. Do you know of anyone in her life who may have wished her harm?"

"I'm sure there are some out there who didn't like her, but I can't think of anyone who would stoop so low as to . . ." Hunter trailed off, obviously deep in thought. "Yes, Mother had the occasional run-in with people who were either jealous of her fortune or didn't care for her personality. But she didn't have enemies. She was always larger than life. Whatever she did, she did it with all her heart. Loved big. Forgave big. Fought big." A small smile tugged at the edges of his mouth. "She was genuine."

"Yes," Luke said. "In our short acquaintance, I found her to be a woman who knew what she wanted."

Hunter grunted. "She never made apologies for who she was, but you always knew where you stood with her. And she had such a heart for others. But I can't imagine anyone wanting to hurt her."

"Hunter, I feel it's my duty to warn you that if news of this gets out before the police solve the mystery, people might assume that you might be involved."

His eyes flashed. "Why? Because I have a record?"

Luke held up his hands. "Unfortunately, yes. From what I gather, you and your mother were on good terms before she died. Otherwise, she wouldn't have updated her will to include you."

"Yes. She was my rock, the one person who truly showed me unconditional love. Even when I messed up—and boy, did I mess up—she refused to give up on me." Hunter wiped tears from his eyes. "Did you know that I yelled at her the day I was arrested? I wanted her to fix things, to wave a magic wand and undo my mess." He chuckled lightly. "But she knew I would never be the man God wanted me to be unless I was forced to grow." He rubbed his forearms. "And yes, I did ask her to forgive me. That's the one thing that's brought me comfort. I made things right with her before she passed."

Luke's chest squeezed with compassion. "That's good."

"As far as the east is from the west," Hunter murmured.

"What was that?"

He shook his head. "It's something the prison chaplain told me, about how God removes sin as far as the east is from the west."

"That's true."

"Maybe not for someone like me. People don't forget."

Luke studied his face, his shoulders hunched. "Not all people will judge you so harshly."

"That was one thing about Mother that always amazed me. She never judged me, not even when I deserved it." Hunter dropped his head in his hands. "I should have appreciated her more."

Luke pondered the reaction. Hunter seemed genuinely upset at his mother's death. "Your mother was excited about your release. And now I imagine it's hard to make a fresh start without a good support system like her around. Has anyone in the family come to visit you?"

"No. Not really," said Hunter. "Alexis texted me a few days ago that we should get together to discuss Mother's funeral arrangements. Sure, she can text but she can't visit." His eyes widened. "Wait. I take that back. My uncle visited yesterday."

"Your uncle?"

"Yes, Victor."

Luke's heart picked up speed. *Victor visited Hunter yesterday?*

Hunter continued, unaware of Luke's musings. "He's my father's brother. Grumpiest man I've ever known. And I've known a few."

"Can you tell me what he said?"

Hunter snorted. "Yelled, more like it. He asked me if I knew anything about Mother's will. Accused me of manipulating her to change it." He lifted his hands in a helpless gesture. "I had no idea what he was raving about—not until you got here, that is. Mother's will never crossed my mind. I want to stand on my own two feet for once."

Luke leaned forward. "Did you tell that to Honey?"

"Of course." He scrubbed the back of his neck. "She kept insisting that she wanted to help me financially, but I would either change the subject or make a joke." Hunter met Luke's eye squarely. "Understand me, Mr. Harris. I didn't want to hurt her more than I already had. As soon as I could, I found myself a job."

"Really? Where?"

"Rotating tires and doing other maintenance work for an automotive shop. It's not glamorous, but it's steady, honest work and it pays the bills."

Luke studied the man before him. He couldn't have killed his mother. He was too focused on improving himself. "You want to show that you've changed. Not only to your mother, but to yourself."

"Yes. Exactly." His shoulders sagged with relief. "It's nice that Mother included me in her will, but the truth is, I don't care about the money. I've learned there are a lot more important things in life. Things that won't rot or vanish with time."

Luke cleared his throat. "Did your uncle say anything more about the will?"

"He asked if I knew anything and demanded I give him some money if I got any. He said my mother would've wanted that. My father too, for that matter. But I'm not so sure. I don't think they liked him much, not that they ever would have said so to Alexis or me."

Interesting.

Glancing at his watch, Luke stood. "Thank you for the chat, but I've taken up enough of your time. Here." He pulled a business card from his wallet and handed it to Hunter. "Feel free to contact me anytime if you have questions about the will. The court will be in touch with you soon to discuss specifics."

Hunter rose and walked with him to the front of the house. "Thank you, Mr. Harris."

Before returning to his office, Luke decided to pay Victor Northcutt a visit. It was best to settle the debate of Honey's will now. He made a quick call to Officer Taylor and let him know of his plan, just in case.

Luke rapped on the door several times before it opened. Victor Northcutt glowered at him from inside the foyer.

"Yes? You need something?" The man's thick eyebrows dipped low as he frowned.

"Mr. Northcutt, I need to spea—"

The door creaked wide as Victor stepped onto the porch. "You're that lawyer, aren't you?"

"Yes sir. I represent Honey and her estate."

The man's demeanor smoothed into a welcoming smile, though it never reached his eyes. "Funny time for a will reading, isn't it?"

"I was at your nephew's house and—"

"Wait a minute. You visited Hunter?"

Luke grimaced at the snarl in the man's tone. "Yes. I needed to speak to him regarding Honey's will."

At the mention of the will, hope flickered across Victor's features. For a moment, Luke regretted that he would be dashing it soon. "I see. And what of it?"

"In her original will, you inherited quite a bit of money," he admitted. Victor grinned. "But now, I'm sorry to tell you, her will doesn't mention you."

Silence pulled as Victor stretched to his full height. "I think I must have misheard you, Mr. Harris. What do you mean by 'doesn't mention'? You mean I'm not in there at all? Explain yourself."

"Honey has not seen fit to leave you anything."

"What? Nothing?"

"No, I—"

But Victor didn't seem interested in listening. His face grew crimson, and his voice shook. "How could she do this to me? It's those brats she calls children, isn't it? They get everything, I take it?"

"I can't give details at this time."

"I bet they do. Mr. Harris, you don't know what it was like to watch George and Honey vacation every year with those kids, always so ungrateful and rude. Each destination was more elaborate than the last. Meanwhile, I was forced to stay home summer after summer, taking care of their home or what have you while they were gone. They let Alexis and Hunter parade around in their name-brand clothes, knowing their excess would have taken care of my needs while I worked two jobs to make ends meet." He picked at the peeling paint of the porch rails. "I did everything to help them and I get nothing for it."

Luke watched the man closely. The image he painted of Honey and George contrasted sharply with what Hunter had told him. But both men stood firm in their convictions. Was the man before him capable of murder? He was certainly bitter.

"Like father like son, though." Victor eyed Luke with stark envy. "You want to know something? My father always favored George. He gave him everything. Left him everything. And I—" He swallowed hard, the Adam's apple bobbing in his throat. "I could never make him happy. It's just like Honey to follow her husband's lead and leave her beloved children everything. Meanwhile, those who really helped her are left in the dirt."

"It's hurtful and unfortunate and unfair," Luke said. "But please, Mr. Northcutt, please realize this is not your fault. It was Honey's decision, what to do with her estate. I'm sure she didn't mean you any harm. She was merely thinking of her children."

Victor clenched and unclenched his fists, and a vein began to throb in his temple. "I've worked my fingers to the bone all my life, while my brother played the part of the family prince. I gave George money I couldn't spare when he needed help most. I thought Honey finally understood my worth and appreciated me. I guess not." He huffed out a harsh breath. "I'm well and truly done with this family. They'll be sorry without Uncle Victor to back them up."

To what lengths would this man go to secure his future? It was clear to Luke that Victor had precious little control over his feelings. Did that extend to his actions as well?

"Mr. Northcutt, you should know that the police are launching an investigation."

Victor gaped at him. "An investigation? Whatever for?"

"Foul play is suspected in Honey's death."

The older man hissed. "Foul play?" His eyes widened. "Wait. Do they think I'm a suspect?"

Luke lifted his chin. "I can't say for sure, but your obsession with Honey's fortune is troubling."

Victor's voice lowered to a growl. "Oh no. Don't you dare. I haven't lived my life being the mud under my brother's shoe only to be falsely accused of his wife's death. I see what this is." He lurched forward and shook his finger near Luke's nose. "It's you. You're after her fortune. You saw Honey's assets and now you're out to do some fancy footwork, accusing her family of murder to clear the way for yourself."

Is the man serious? "That doesn't even make sense, Mr. Northcutt. Legally, I have no control over Honey's wishes. I am simply trying to get to the bottom of—"

Victor took a step closer, breath heaving. "You're no cop. You have no right to step foot on my property."

Unease crawled up Luke's spine.

"You've said your piece. Now get out of my life," Victor snapped. He stomped back into his house and slammed the door in Luke's face.

Luke trudged back to his car. The man was upset, understandably, but something more colored his tone. Annoyance? Fear? Revenge? He couldn't place it.

His phone buzzed. Rolling the tension from his muscles, he pulled the phone from his pocket and glimpsed the text message lighting up the screen.

Mr. Harris, it's Stella. A friend told me she saw Antonio's show at The Bad Punchline last night and his act isn't getting any better. No mother-in-law jokes this time, but that's only this once. Is there no way to talk reason into him?

Luke chuckled dryly. At least he was helpful to someone. He decided to call the woman on his hands-free system as he drove. He hoped she'd be open to discussing Antonio's worries and meeting again—and in turn help him regain some of his sanity.

18

Meagan

Meagan padded into the kitchen and rubbed her bleary eyes. *What a night.* Sleep hadn't come easily. Her thoughts about Honey Northcutt and the local robberies had run circles through her mind all night long.

She still wasn't sure what to think about Honey's death. It was so cruel if she had been murdered. So pointless. She knew Luke, Piper, and the police had that matter well in hand, but thoughts of the woman's situation wouldn't rest. Neither would news of the robberies rising in their community. Why did they bother her so much? No one had targeted her shop. But she felt for the store owners experiencing the thefts. They were like her, trying to make a living doing what they loved. She brushed away the musings before they made her miserable for her workday. That wouldn't do.

Luckily, Hash Brown trotted into the kitchen with a doggy smile on his face. Meagan beamed, her mood instantly lifting as she watched him head to his food bowl, no doubt trusting that his meal would be there soon.

"Hungry this morning, Hash Brown?" The pup raced in circles, too excited to stay still as she pulled his bag of dog food from the counter. She poured some into his bowl and scratched behind his ears. "Enjoy your breakfast, and I'll do the same."

Hash Brown buried his nose in the dish, munching loudly. Meagan grinned and opened the refrigerator. A cup of coffee with cream and a smoothie would be a perfect start to her day.

She pulled Greek yogurt from the fridge and tore off the lid, intending to add a dollop to her smoothie for a protein boost. But something told her to taste it first. Grabbing a spoon from the silverware drawer, she scooped some up and grimaced as soon as it touched her tongue. It had gone bad.

She hurried to wash away the taste. Then she turned to the yogurt container, checking the expiration date. *It should be good for another week.*

Confused, Meagan opened the fridge again and stuck her hand inside. It wasn't as cold as it should have been. She groaned and pulled out the perishables one by one. Meat, milk, leftovers—all of them would need to go.

Of course, I get my week's groceries and then *the refrigerator decides to bail.* She wrinkled her nose and tossed the food into the trash.

Beside her, Hash Brown whined, sensing that she was unhappy.

"At least one of us gets breakfast." She dialed her grandmother's number.

"Hello?" Nell's voice always had a sunshiny quality to it despite the day's circumstances.

"Hey, Nan. Any chance I could borrow some of your milk for my morning coffee?"

"Of course, dear. Come grab it anytime. No chance to get groceries?"

"Not exactly." Meagan tried to figure out how to break the news. Living in Nell's carriage house meant the large Federal-style home was a stone's throw away from Meagan's home nestled in the expansive backyard. Nell always worried about appliances dying and maintenance issues, taking on the responsibility of landlord—expenses she didn't need to worry over in her retirement years. Meagan fixed most of the small issues herself, never wanting to make things harder for her, but today's issue might call for a professional. "I hate to tell you this, but the refrigerator is out."

Nell sighed. "It was bound to happen sooner or later. It's an older model. Do you think it's on the fritz, or does it need to be completely replaced?"

"Not sure." Meagan regarded the humming appliance before moving to fill Hash Brown's water bowl. "It's running, but it feels like a Southern summer in there right now."

Chuckling, Nell shifted something. The rustling crackled over the line. "I want you to tell me if it needs replacing. I can handle it, Meagan."

"No way. My fridge, my problem."

"My carriage house," Nell said with finality. "I'm doing fine financially. Your grandpa saw to that."

Meagan knew her grandmother spoke truth. After Meagan's grandfather, Lincoln Poe, left the navy, he'd used his extensive knowledge of boats to open a marina, which then blossomed into a business that grew to multiple locations. He and Nell had retired comfortably. When he passed away ten years ago, Nell took on sole management of all the finances and maintenance of both their large home and the small carriage house in the backyard. She had the means to care for their property, but Meagan didn't have the heart to see her grandmother squander her resources at Meagan's expense.

Meagan tried to negotiate. "How about if it's a simple fix, you pay for it, but if it needs replacing, I'll do it."

"Switch the scenario around and we have a deal."

Meagan propped a hand on her hip. "You aren't going to let me win this one, are you?"

"No, dear. This is when I tell you to listen to your elders."

Nell's laugh caused Meagan to smile. "Okay," she relented. "I'll at least call a repairman and let you know what he says."

"All right, dear. My kitchen is open if you need anything. In fact, feel free to share a bite with me now. I always love your company."

Meagan jogged up the stairs to her bedroom to search for her shoes. "You help me at Rose Cottage Books and now have to deal with me invading your breakfast time." Kneeling by her bed, she peered under the frame with the phone still pressed to her ear and spied the wayward sneakers.

"Oh, you know I would keep you in my pocket if I could get away with it."

"I don't think I'd fit, but that might be the only thing stopping you." Unearthing the shoes from beneath the bed, she settled on the floor to put them on, cradling the phone between her head and her shoulder. Not the most comfortable way to chat, but it worked. "By the way, what are you having?"

"*We* are having French toast."

"I'll be there soon."

She hung up and trotted back down the stairs, whistling for Hash Brown, who bounded toward the door. The little dog knew better than to miss out on the fun.

As soon as she entered the main house, the aroma of maple syrup and cinnamon tickled her nose. Her grandmother stood on the diamond-patterned wooden floor in front of the stove, flipping thick slices of toast with practiced ease.

"Hi, Meagan." She scooped two golden pieces of French toast onto a plate and began dunking two new slices into an egg mixture for which Meagan had been trying to get the recipe for years. Nell pointed to some dishes on the table. "There's fruit, syrup, and powdered sugar waiting for you. Cute pj's."

"Thanks, Nan." Kissing Nell's soft cheek, she took the plate gladly. "I snagged these as soon as I saw them. A bookstore owner needs a pair of pajamas with the names of famous opening lines plastered on them." She peered into the bowls on the table. "You put out extra powdered sugar. You know me well."

Eyes dancing, Nell laid her own French toast in the pan. "Never did see such a mound of white than when you got that funnel cake at the fair last year."

Meagan sprinkled slices of strawberry on her plate. "Funnel cake requires powdered sugar. It's a crucial part of the experience."

"Only yours are two parts sugar, one part funnel cake, which makes me think the experience you actually want is the sugar, and the funnel cake is merely a vessel."

"You got me." Meagan slid into a dining room chair with a grin. "But it makes for a happy day."

Hash Brown situated himself underneath the table, ready to nab the smallest crumb that fell.

Nell soon joined her granddaughter, and after offering a soft prayer of thanks, she speared a bite of her French toast with relish. "Your day is off to an interesting start, I'd say." Her attention turned to her food. "Mmm. Nothing else can hit the spot like this."

Meagan smiled around her fork and swallowed. "Be honest, though. Are there any bad breakfast foods?"

Nell shook her head. "Not a one." The snowy-haired woman tossed something under the table with an impish grin, where Hash Brown could be heard gobbling it down.

"You know I don't give him table scraps," Meagan protested.

"That wasn't French toast, dear. It was one of the treats I keep especially for him." She patted the pocket of her cardigan. "You know that whenever he comes over, I tuck some in here. I think it makes him happy."

Meagan poked at a berry with her fork. "Speaking of happy, or maybe not so happy, do you happen to know anything about Victor Northcutt?" Not one for overt gossip, she left out the fact that Luke had texted her and Piper yesterday evening about his visit to the man.

"Northcutt?" Nell wiped her lips with a napkin. "As in brother to George Northcutt?"

"Yes."

Nell shrugged. "He worked for a while for your grandpa Lincoln after we opened the marina."

"Really?" Meagan chewed slowly, digesting the information. "What was he like? I mean, as an employee."

Nell sipped her orange juice, her expression thoughtful. "He worked hard, but he wasn't the best with people. He had definite ideas about how things should be and why." She picked up her fork again and ran a bite of toast through a puddle of syrup. "You know your grandfather, though. He had a way of soothing tempers. When Victor would get hot under the collar, Lincoln would sit down with him and let him vent. Everything was fine after that." She frowned, her gaze sharp. "Why do you ask?"

Meagan hesitated. *How much should I tell?* "I saw him at Island Market. He was having a rather heated conversation with the deli worker." She focused on cutting off the perfect bite of toast. "And Luke was trying to locate him earlier."

A smile crossed Nell's lips. "Luke?"

Meagan rolled her eyes. "Don't start that again."

"Start what, dear? I saw you two at book club Saturday." Nell winked. "There's a spark there."

Meagan gave her grandmother a reproachful look. There had been nothing to see. Book club had gone normally on Saturday—a happy time despite the tense circumstances surrounding the town—and Luke had been nothing but kind to her, offering jokes and commentary about the book club book. If there was anything there, it was friendship.

Nell's smile slipped into a wistful expression. "Don't let memories of Carl ruin your future."

Meagan swallowed hard and set down her fork. "It's not Carl. I really am over him, Nan. It's just that . . ." She trailed off.

"What, dear?" Nell prompted gently.

"What if it happens again? What if I open up my heart to someone, and it's broken like it was before?"

Nell took her hand. "I've discovered that 'what-ifs' are a terrible way to live your life—or rather, to avoid living it. It allows another's mistakes to affect your future. Instead of thinking ahead to everything that might go wrong, focus on the now. Build friendships. Concentrate on connection. Take each day one moment at a time." She let go of Meagan's hand and went back to her breakfast. "Sometimes it's one breath at a time."

"One breath at a time," Meagan echoed. "I like that. And it's doable."

"The best advice in life usually is." Nell pulled another dog treat from her pocket and tossed it to Hash Brown.

Meagan shook her head but couldn't hide a grin. "I'm going to leave him with you permanently if you keep it up."

Nell cooed to Hash Brown, who wiggled with joy and leaned against her chair, clearly hoping for more treats or affection. "Much as I love spoiling my grandpuppy, we both know he would never choose me over you."

After finishing breakfast and clearing the dishes, Meagan waved goodbye and headed back across the lawn to finish getting ready for the day. She donned jeans, a lavender shirt, and a gray cardigan before driving to Rose Cottage Books.

The first item on the agenda was to call a refrigerator repairman.

Meagan had barely unlocked the bookstore and flicked on the lights in the stockroom when she sensed a presence behind her. She tensed, wondering if it was another raccoon, but dismissed the thought. Raccoons didn't wait patiently.

"Good morning," sang out a familiar voice.

Meagan spun around.

Piper stood by the front counter, a simple purse hanging from one shoulder today rather than her usual assortment of bags.

Meagan went to meet her. "Hi, Piper. I must've been so lost in my thoughts that I didn't hear the door open. You're here early. What did you do, wait in your car and stake out the shop until I opened?"

"Yes," Piper deadpanned. Strolling to the fudge display stocked by Pirate Treasures Candy, she scanned the collection. "No more peanut butter fudge?"

Meagan glanced over her shoulder as she carried a waiting package to the register. "Sold out for now."

"Rats." Piper browsed the other options, but apparently nothing else tempted her. "Sorry I missed book club Saturday. Anything new and exciting happen?"

Meagan powered on the point-of-sale register. "Book club was fun. You were missed. As for new, I've been trying to solve the mystery of the robbers on the block. Still no luck tracking anyone down. But get this." She propped her elbows on the counter. "We had visitors the other day. Two raccoons in our trash cans."

Piper's eyes widened. "Did Hash Brown give them an earful?"

"You bet."

At the sound of his name, Hash Brown poked his head out of the mouth of his shark-shaped bed behind the counter.

"That reminds me. We had an incident with our trash this morning," Piper said.

Meagan tensed. "You did?"

"Yep."

"What happened?"

"Ulysses started barking early, around five. Jim let him outside and went back to bed, thinking it was nothing more than the call of nature. When he got up thirty minutes later, there was trash scattered all over the yard. It took us ages to get everything cleaned up." Piper rolled her eyes. "It didn't help that Ulysses got into some peanut butter I tossed. Poor thing had stains all over his fur. I had to give him a bath."

"I can't imagine trying to give a dog that big and with that much fur a bath."

"It's not easy," Piper assured her. "Anyway, Jim swore he saw raccoons scampering away when he went outside, but I think Ulysses wanted a snack and took advantage of the situation."

"If it's raccoons, sounds like they're everywhere these days."

Piper nodded. "Jim heard there have been more than usual this year."

"Guess we'll have to be more diligent about keeping the trash contained."

"And keeping Ulysses inside. He's up on his shots and everything, but I still don't want to risk it. Have you had any other adventures lately?"

"If you call my refrigerator going out and all my food spoiling an 'adventure,' sure." Meagan explained about her refrigerator dilemma, starting with the yogurt, while Piper clucked in sympathy.

"That's terrible, but I'm sure it'll be worked out in no time. Maybe a guy friend can help out somehow," her friend said with a twinkle in her eye. "Speaking of which, do you know what's going on with Luke? I heard about Honey's autopsy and his visit with Victor, but any news on Honey's boyfriend?"

"Yes," Meagan said. "On Friday, Luke met Kevin Chambers at the marina and heard a little about his relationship with Honey."

"Really?" Piper's brows lifted. "And?"

"Kevin was pretty vague about everything, but he got a phone call while they were talking. Luke could hear Alexis Northcutt on the other end. She later told Luke she's never liked Kevin and hired a private detective to check him out."

Piper inhaled sharply. "Did the detective find anything?"

Meagan pursed her lips. "Only that Chambers isn't Kevin's last name. It's York."

"Ooh." Piper rubbed her hands together. "That's a juicy tidbit. But why change his name? It makes no sense."

"Luke thinks he's got something to hide."

"Hmm. Hide what, though? He likely won't inherit anything from Honey's estate. Not as family, anyway. They weren't married."

"I suppose that's for the police and Luke to figure out. I don't know. Maybe Kevin has nothing to do with it at all."

Piper's eyes swept the book club sign at the end of the counter. "Anything else?"

Meagan used a box cutter to open a fresh shipment of books. "I'm a terrible liar."

Piper laughed. "Yes, but it's endearing."

Meagan handed Piper a book. "Help me shelve?"

"Sure." Piper shadowed Meagan to the best-seller section. "What makes you a terrible liar?"

"Luke was telling me how he had been trained to spot deception. I tested him and he sniffed out my lie like that." She snapped her fingers and reached for another volume.

"Deception, huh?" Piper carried a stack of books to the best-seller display. "Sounds like a skill I need to learn." She grinned. "Especially when Jim claims he didn't eat the last doughnut."

Meagan giggled. "It goes both ways. Don't forget—I've seen you squirm when Jim asks you if yet another online order is waiting on the front porch."

"Fair enough."

"How is your beauty column, by the way?"

Piper straightened a few books. "Cooper has ordered more supplies.

I'm going back to online delivery. I guess the secret-shopper experience was a one-time thing."

"I see," Meagan said. "I thought that could have been the start of a more investigative angle to the column for you."

Piper shrugged. "It wasn't meant to be this time. I'll hope for the odd assignment here and there, and be happy with the bites I get when they come—be that through work or through the fun you, Luke, and the rest of the book club go through. Besides, I get to keep telling the truth about what I write, and that's what matters most to me."

"As long as you're happy."

"I am," Piper said.

"There's nothing better than that."

"I think we're all pretty lucky in that respect—Olivia, Avery, you, me, and Luke. We all enjoy our jobs."

"True. I only hope Luke's not questioning his happiness after the clients he's had lately."

Piper raised an eyebrow at her. "Are you kidding? He loves this stuff. You can see it in his face when he talks about it. It's tough, but he's tougher. He likes the challenge."

Meagan nodded. "I do hope you're right and that he's not deceiving us by masking his true feelings."

"That man couldn't deceive you if he tried," Piper said with a snort. "He's too interested in being your friend."

Meagan felt her cheeks warm, but she said nothing. *I like being his friend too.*

19

Luke

Luke sat inside Aunt Maisie's and absently stirred his coffee. The spoon clinked softly against the ceramic cup. His thoughts swirled with the black brew, spinning but going nowhere. After placating Stella following her desperate text the day before, he'd spent the remainder of the day contemplating Honey's estate and possible murder. As usual, those thoughts didn't vanish with sleep.

"Doing okay over here?" The waitress had appeared with a coffeepot.

He offered a wan smile. "I'm okay. Just stewing."

The waitress raised an eyebrow. "Sounds like an unproductive way to spend the day." She jabbed a pencil into her fluffy brown coif. "I've seen happier faces on hound dogs."

"I'm having trouble sorting through a problem." He set down his cup and rubbed his temples. "I suppose I'm trying to put a puzzle together that doesn't want to fit."

"Know what I do when a puzzle piece won't fit? I bend it until I get it to work."

Luke laughed. "And how does the picture look when you've finished?"

She grinned. "Sometimes, not so good. With other puzzles, the overall picture is so lovely no one notices. Like those impressionist paintings by—what's his name?"

"Monet?"

"Yes, him." She topped off his cup. "The point is, when the picture isn't clear, sometimes you have to experiment with the pieces.

Especially when the final piece you need is missing."

The thought gave him pause. He was indeed missing something when it came to Honey Northcutt's death, but what?

"Holler if you need anything," she said, then headed to another table.

Left alone once more, Luke steepled his fingers and sorted through the pieces he had at hand, wondering if the police were doing the same. Alexis, the housekeeper's conversation with Piper, Hunter, Kevin, Victor Northcutt and his soured relationship with his family. He was circling around the truth but was still unable to see it. *I need the last missing piece.*

He'd called Officer Taylor after leaving Victor's house. The police officer had whistled when he learned of Victor's reaction.

"Okay. We're working on a formal investigation here, and now that I have this information, I'll do some more digging. As for you, go about your everyday life. There's no need to bring extra trouble down on your head. Or mine for letting a private citizen do my work."

Luke shifted in his seat. Officer Taylor seemed worried that Luke's efforts would botch the investigation somehow. But Luke couldn't sit still and wait. He wanted to help.

After another sip of coffee, he pulled out his phone and did a search for *ethylene glycol.* Piper had told him what she knew, but he wanted more information. *And,* he reasoned, *I can't mess up an investigation by searching the Internet.*

Tapping on the first authoritative link he found, he read: *Ethylene glycol is used for two main purposes: to manufacture polyester and as a component in coolant and antifreeze.*

Coolant and antifreeze? He pondered that and read on.

This compound is a poison readily found in homes and garages. It is odorless and has a sweet taste. It is nontoxic, but the human body metabolizes it into toxins that damage the kidneys and other vital organs. Slurring and stumbling are common after ingesting ethylene glycol.

Luke leaned back in his chair. The symptoms matched Piper's research and were consistent with the housekeeper's account of Honey's odd behavior the evening of her death. But the timing of her will revisions bothered Luke. It was so close to the day she died. Was it planned? Or mere coincidence?

From what he'd heard and witnessed, he thought Honey was incapable of taking her own life. But who would poison the woman? And why?

He picked up his phone once again and sent a text to Meagan and Piper.

Still thinking about Hunter and Victor Northcutt.

Piper was the first to respond. *What about them?*

He reflected on the men before typing his answer. He had no idea what Hunter had been like in the past, but the man he'd chatted with seemed genuine and thoughtful, a guy he could easily be friends with.

Hunter is very hurt by his mother's passing and recently turned his life around. I don't think he's suspicious, but it's odd that his uncle visited him shortly before I did.

Piper texted back. *Agreed.*

Hunter said Victor accused him of attempting to change Honey's will by manipulating her.

A text dinged from Meagan. *When you met with Victor, how did he act?*

Angry. Told me to stay out of his business.

Wow, Meagan wrote.

Nice guy, Piper added.

He smiled, picturing the two women ready to jump into the fray. *Not surprising, considering I told him he wouldn't inherit anything. And then there's the matter of Honey's autopsy.*

Several dots drifted across his screen before Meagan's reply popped up. *How do you think the poison got into her system?*

Ingestion. Nothing else suspicious showed up on the toxicology report.

Piper jumped back in. *Sorry. Cooper called with another beauty assignment. I guess the logical thing would be to find out who saw Honey on the day of her death.*

Absolutely, Luke thought. A strange sense of expectation coursed through his veins. *Who had Honey seen that day?* He sorted through what he knew of her schedule.

She had visited friends for a card game. After that, she had seen the housekeeper, and possibly Alexis. *Who else?*

Then it came to him. The friend who had driven her home—and who happened to be in the new will.

Luke tapped out a message. *Got an idea. Going to talk with DeeDee Davis. She drove Honey home from a card game the day she died. Keep you posted.*

He pocketed his phone and left a generous tip next to his coffee on the table, then raced toward his car.

Maybe DeeDee can help me put the picture together. Or maybe I'm bending a puzzle piece to make it fit.

After a brief stop at his office to retrieve the court notice and confirm DeeDee's address, he raced toward her house. Or tried to. Traffic crawled through town—a sign of the impending tourist season—and when the GPS announced that he had arrived, he gave a silent cheer.

Colorful flowers in terra-cotta pots clustered around the yellow country-style home. The grass was freshly cut, the green clippings gathered at the edge of the yard. Black garbage bags were piled in a heap by the street. Cut limbs and clippings peeked out from the ties pinched at the tops. Apparently, DeeDee was a meticulous gardener. Luke hoped she could be as exacting in recalling Honey's last day.

The older woman was out front watering purple petunias, red roses, and pink hydrangeas. She raised her head when he parked the car and climbed out. "It's Mr. Harris, right?"

"Yes ma'am." He strolled up the drive, admiring the nostalgic feel of DeeDee's house. It was like being back at his grandmother's.

Shoving his hands in his pockets, he approached the smiling woman. "Sorry to drop in on you like this. I needed to contact you about some things related to Honey's estate."

Her brows lifted. "Me? I don't think I have much to offer, but I'm always happy for a visit. Come on in and I'll get you some cookies and lemonade." She ushered him inside to a sunny sitting room, complete with floral patterns on the curtains and sofa. Dog toys decorated the end tables. A coffee table displayed a small stack of magazines. The scent of baked goods wafted through the air. "I have sugar cookies, snickerdoodles, and oatmeal cookies fresh out of the oven."

Luke felt his stomach growling suddenly. "I like all of them, but please don't go to any trouble for me." He settled on the plush sofa, trying not to lean against the giant lace throw draped over the back.

"No trouble," DeeDee insisted as she continued to the kitchen. "I enjoy having someone to spoil now and again."

Luke pondered which questions he should ask. *What line will lead to the missing puzzle piece?*

DeeDee reemerged with snickerdoodles and a tall glass of lemonade. She handed them to him with a smile.

"Now, what is this business about Honey's will?"

He took a bite of the cookie and grinned as it melted in his mouth. "These are so good."

She beamed. "That recipe has been in my family for generations. Now, how can I help about poor Honey?"

"Part of the process is settling all of Honey's assets in probate court. It's standard practice. The court has asked me to contact all the beneficiaries who should be present at the court for the final hearing."

He smiled gently. "You are one of those beneficiaries, DeeDee. I am talking to the others who should be present as well."

"Oh my." Her brows pinched. "But what does this mean?"

"It means Honey left something to you, but I'm not at liberty to say what until the hearing. Everything must go through the probate court first." He handed her the note saying as much.

DeeDee swallowed, tears gathering in her eyes as she examined the paper in her hands. "That's just like Honey, you know. Thinking about her friends. Even on the last day of her life she was thinking about everyone else."

"I'm sure losing your friend wasn't easy," Luke said, watching her carefully.

DeeDee sniffed. "I never imagined Honey would leave us so quickly." She twisted her hands in her lap. "I remember the day she died, she arrived in the nick of time for our weekly card game. We always meet at three o'clock to play spades."

"Spades? I've never played."

"You should." Her face brightened with the change of topic. "We have such fun, and it's different every time. Keeps us from getting bored."

"Who is 'we'?"

"Myself, Honey, Gloria Ludwig, Paula Griep, and Cynthia Mulligan."

He committed those names to memory as best he could. "Please, go on."

She wiped away a nonexistent speck of dust from the coffee table. "Sometimes we play as teams and other times as single players."

"Which was it the day that Honey passed?"

"Hmm." She tapped her lower lip. "I believe we played teams. Paula couldn't come that day—watching grandkids, you know—so Cynthia and I were on a team, and Honey and Gloria made up the other."

He grunted and took more mental notes, planning to pass this information along to Officer Taylor as soon as he could. It wouldn't hurt for the police to talk to all the ladies of this card group, including Paula. Although the woman hadn't been able to attend, she might have some insight into Honey's past that the others overlooked. "What's the object of spades?"

DeeDee chuckled. "It's such a hoot. Everyone bids on how many tricks they think they can take from their opponents. When the game starts, you aim to win that many tricks. The spades suit is always trump."

Luke frowned. "How did Honey perform at spades that last day? Was she confused at all? Unable to focus?"

"Not at all. In fact, she and Gloria clobbered Cynthia and me."

"How long did you play?"

She shrugged. "A couple of hours, as usual. After the other two left, Honey sat here with me and chatted for a good while."

"Anything specific on her mind?"

"Not really. Family. How she wanted to redecorate her bedroom. Things like that."

Someone planning to redecorate her bedroom likely didn't have suicide on her mind. "She mentioned her family to you?"

"She always called me her best friend and would ask for advice about Alexis and Hunter," DeeDee explained. "Those two worried her to death. I was kind of her confidant when it came to them."

"What did she say about them that day?"

The older woman picked up a cookie. "She kept saying that she'd witnessed a big change in both of them. I'm not sure I see it. Alexis is as spoiled as she ever was, and Hunter still needs to earn back everyone's trust. It will take time, but it will help folks see if he's truly changed or not."

"How long did you talk?"

She broke off a piece of the cookie and ate it. "About two hours or so. I remember thinking it was close to seven and wondering if I should make her something to eat. I mean, we'd had coffee and cake during the card game, but it was getting late."

"That's a long time to visit."

"Not uncommon for us. We could talk until the sun rose."

He smiled. "That's a mark of true friendship, much like your driving her home that night. How did that come about?"

"She said she wasn't feeling well. I assumed she was getting another one of her migraines. She had them frequently, you know."

No, he didn't, but he made a quick note of it. "That's too bad."

"Poor woman had them a couple of times a month. They really took it out of her for a day or so." She took another bite of her cookie and swallowed. "It wasn't unusual for one of us ladies to drive her home if a migraine developed. She would come back to get her car the next day. I assumed that's all it was." Her chin quivered. "I had no idea that would be the last time I saw her."

He patted her hand. "I'm sorry."

DeeDee gave him a watery smile. "Thank you. She's very missed."

The two sat in silence for several moments, Luke contemplating all he'd been told, and DeeDee sniffling quietly.

Once he thought the woman had calmed down, Luke stood to leave. "You've been a huge help, Mrs. Davis. I have to get going now. Thank you so much for your time. You'll receive more details about the court date for Honey's will soon. And thank you for the delicious cookies. Mind if I take one for the road?"

"I insist on it. I'm always making something in the kitchen. It's a way I can give back to others." She handed him several cookies. "Besides, a young man like you needs nourishment. I'm sure you're very busy as a lawyer, and you have to keep your strength up."

He thanked her and left, his brain churning over the information. Nothing sounded particularly out of place with DeeDee's story, but it still felt like something was missing.

Trees and shrubs blurred past as he drove down one block, then another. Colonial homes gave way to modest subdivisions. He peered at the gas station on the side of the road. *Haven't I seen that station before?* He glanced around. Landmarks and houses tugged at his memory. *I have been here. This is Victor Northcutt's neighborhood.*

The last thing he wanted to do was run into the man again, especially after yesterday. He searched for a place to turn around.

Taking a deep breath, he drove past Victor's residence and nearly slammed on the brakes. Alexis stood outside with the man, but instead of the vitriol he had witnessed last week at Honey's home, the two of them had their heads together, deep in conversation.

He shifted in his seat. *Are they reconciling? Or plotting?*

Victor Northcutt's ire would only increase if he learned Luke was driving by and peering into his affairs. Forcing his attention back to the road, he reached the end of the cul-de-sac, rounded the circle, and hit the gas. But his thoughts remained on what he was leaving behind.

His phone rang, and he hit the button to connect to the car's sound system. "Hello?"

"Luke? This is Avery Sheridan, from book club."

"Hey, Avery. How are you?"

"I'm good, but listen. I was down near the marina again and guess who I saw?"

His phone buzzed with an incoming text, a photo. Forcing his attention back to the road, he tightened his grip on the steering wheel. "I'm driving, so I can't really look at that right now. But is it Kevin?"

Excitement colored her voice. "Yep. And guess who's with him?"

"Who?"

"Some new redheaded girlfriend," Avery replied. "Why is he with another woman when Honey died less than two weeks ago?"

A jolt sliced through his veins. "I don't know. How did they act?"

"Smiling. Joking. This new lady was hanging on his every word."

Luke ground his jaw. *What is Kevin up to?* "Troubling for sure. Thanks for the heads-up, Avery."

They ended the call. He braked at a stoplight and checked his buzzing phone again. A new text lit up the screen.

Hey, Mr. Harris. This is Alexis Northcutt. Can we meet up sometime soon? I need to talk about Mother.

Odd timing. He'd seen Alexis talking with Victor mere moments ago. Had Victor prompted her, or had their meeting been nothing more than burying the past?

The light changed, and he drove on. How would he ever solve the puzzle of Honey's death when more pieces kept crowding the table?

20

Meagan

Meagan hummed to herself as she dusted the shelves at Rose Cottage Books. Straightening from her crouched position, she observed her handiwork and released a satisfied sigh. She didn't think she would ever tire of the smell of new books, chocolate, and coffee that permeated this place. Dulcet jazz tones played over the sound system, adding to the relaxing air of the shop.

Despite the pleasant atmosphere, Meagan's mind was anything but settled. The unresolved thefts left her wondering if her own bookshop would be next. Should she talk to Larry about purchasing a security system? The thought left her ill at ease. She didn't want to live in fear, but neither could she ignore a growing problem.

Luke's news about Victor unsettled her too. Luke had sounded upset when he'd called about that. She wondered what she could do to help him. *Not much but pray.* But she knew that even a small act like that could accomplish great things. Her thoughts rewound to the weekend once more. Book club had offered a chance for them to relax, to momentarily forget the troubles of the week. Sunday she'd worshiped at Trinity Christian Church, one of her favorite activities.

Yet even there she'd been unable to escape thoughts of Honey Northcutt. Pastor Russ Miller had announced that Honey's funeral would be held there soon, twisting a knot in Meagan's stomach. As far as she, Luke, and Piper knew, the police were still investigating the woman's death. Could she be buried? Meagan decided to pray for answers for all—soon.

The sound of the door opening caught Meagan's attention. She tossed the dust rag into the bucket of cleaning supplies and went to greet the customer. An older woman with fluffy gray curls and a winsome smile tugged her purse strap higher on her shoulder as she walked past the front display.

"Welcome to Rose Cottage Books," said Meagan.

"Thank you. Don't let me keep you from your work. I'm browsing."

A bark issued from the back before Hash Brown appeared. He approached the woman and tilted his head.

A smile broke across the woman's face. "Aren't you the cutest thing?"

Hash Brown's body wiggled, and he scampered to meet a new friend. The woman reached down and scratched his head, murmuring as he leaned into her touch.

"Do you like dogs?" Meagan asked.

"I love them. This little guy reminds me of my dog, Oreo." She sniffed. "Poor pup."

Meagan took a step forward. "Is he ill?"

The woman knelt and let Hash Brown lick her cheek. "Sweet boy." She looked up. "No, Oreo is no longer with us. He was a black-and-white miniature border collie. Fluffy, playful, and smart as a whip. But one day, he got into my late husband's car chemicals."

Meagan's heart wrung. "I'm so sorry."

The woman sniffed again and rose. "Thank you. The whole incident was very sad. I miss him dearly."

Meagan glanced at Hash Brown, who stared adoringly at her with his big brown eyes. The woman's melancholy magnified her own gratitude for her faithful companion. Squatting, she scooped him into her arms. She would make sure to spoil him a little extra today.

"Is there anything I can help you with?"

"I hadn't been in here before and wanted to peruse the latest cookbooks. Don't mind me."

Meagan could understand wanting to get a feel for a new shop without someone following her around. "Please let me know if you need anything."

"I will. Thank you."

After the guest wandered toward the nonfiction section, Meagan carried Hash Brown back to where she'd been cleaning. Voices rang out across the store.

"Why, Nell Poe, how nice to see you again."

"DeeDee, what a lovely surprise. Your smile always makes me feel better."

Meagan paused. *DeeDee? Is that the woman Luke wanted to speak to?* She had just leaned in to hear more when her phone buzzed, signaling an incoming call. She answered it. "Hello?"

"Miss Poe? This is Eddie with Al's Auto and Motor repair shop. I hear you got a question about your refrigerator."

Right. She'd nearly forgotten she'd left a message there after Piper left this morning. "Yes. Thank you for calling me back, Eddie. I woke up to discover my refrigerator not working like it should. There was barely any cool air circulating, even though the motor was running. Any ideas on what I should do?"

"Hmm." She could picture the man rubbing his chin as he thought. "Adding some coolant could help. If not, you'll likely need a new one. I can come out this afternoon at three to give it a try." She could hear the sound of rustling papers. "My schedule is pretty tight until then. Ah, actually, maybe I should pencil you in for tomorrow instead. Don't know if I'll be able to stop by and grab the chemicals at the shop."

"I can probably do that part if it'll help you." She wandered to her office desk and retrieved a notepad. "What should I look for?"

"Ethylene glycol."

Meagan froze. *The same substance found in Honey's system?*

Scribbling down the words, she asked, "Do you have it in stock?"

"Not sure. Come to think of it, we might be out." Meagan heard him tapping his pen on the other end of the line. "Yeah, we're out. One of our guys must have sold some last week. Folks never know when they'll need it. A new order should be coming in within an hour or two, though. Still want to swing by later today in case we get it in?"

"Yes, I'll do that." Meagan wanted to have her refrigerator functional again sooner rather than later.

"Good deal. If the shipment doesn't come in today, it should be tomorrow."

"Thanks."

"Give me your address and I'll run out to your place around three or so tomorrow."

After reciting directions to the carriage house, Meagan thanked him for his help and ended the call. She cast a glance toward the front room, but DeeDee had already left.

Her mind whirled. Someone in Nantucket had purchased ethylene glycol within the past week or so. Right around the time Honey had died. If there was a way to track down who had purchased ethylene glycol in that time span . . .

"Hi, Meagan." Nell poked her head around the doorframe. "I'm heading home. Hattie should be here in about five minutes. Hear anything about your refrigerator?"

"They suggested I get coolant, but they're out right now. I'm supposed to run by there in a bit and check on a new shipment, though."

"There's no rush, at least not on my part. You can always take meals with me until it's working again. But I know how you like your routine and those green smoothies in the morning. Want me to take Hash Brown back to the house?"

She smiled at the pup resting on the blanket in the corner. "He'd probably be happy to get out and about. Will you be working in the garden?"

"Of course. That is, unless a storm blows in." Nell peered past her through the window. Thick charcoal clouds rolled in ominous puffs, snuffing out the sunlight.

"All right. Thank you." She crouched and gently scratched the dog's head to wake him. "Hash Brown, Nan is going to take you home for a bit. Outside time."

At the word *outside*, he bounded to his feet and yipped. Meagan fastened a leash to his collar and handed it to Nell. "Thanks, Nan. I'll stop in and get him when I'm done for the day."

"No rush." Nell rubbed Hash Brown's ear. "We're going to play in the garden, aren't we? And we're not going to dig up my flowers this time, are we?"

As the two left, the door opened again, and a mother with two young children stepped inside. Meagan waved through the glass window in her office. The mother waved back as she herded her kids to the children's section. To Meagan's delight, both headed straight for the array of puzzles and picture books by the ark. Meagan smiled to herself, thinking the mother would likely soon visit the fudge display for a boost of sugar.

Picking up her tablet, she doodled with one finger on the blank screen before writing the word *mystery* along the top. She bit her lip. *How many other people purchased coolant in Nantucket on a daily basis? If I can narrow it down … And how odd that DeeDee visited for the first time and happened to mention how she'd lost her dog.*

She shook her head. She was jumping to conclusions. Purchasing a common chemical didn't make someone a murderer. This investigation was making her paranoid.

Still, the lingering suspicion niggled.

"Oh, I'm so sorry!"

The apology across the room pulled Meagan from her thoughts. She hurried out of her office toward the sound in time to see a blonde woman with a lot of jewelry trying to wipe a stain off her bright-pink blouse.

Something about her was familiar. Meagan squinted. *Is that Alexis Northcutt?* She certainly resembled the woman flooding Piper's social media feed.

"Is there anything I can do?" asked the mother who had brought in her young children. Glancing around, she grabbed a wad of napkins from the fudge counter and handed them to the other woman. "I wanted to give them a sample of the fudge that's out on the counter. If I had known Silas would brush against you and leave that stain—"

The woman smiled tightly. "No. Really. It's fine."

Snagging a pile of wet wipes tucked behind the register, Meagan hurried forward and held them out. "Here. These should help." She kept her voice soothing, praying the mother wouldn't berate herself for the small mistake—and that the other woman wouldn't berate her either.

Up close, Meagan had her answer. The woman in pink was indeed Alexis.

Alexis took a wet wipe and dabbed at the smudge on her shirt. "Thank you." Her words were kind, but her voice was strained. "I think I'll go back to my browsing."

Shooting the mother an apologetic look, Meagan followed Alexis into the romance section. "Can I help you find something today?"

Alexis peered over the titles, her lips pursed. "I don't know. My friends think I need to start reading, but it's so *dull*." Picking up one of the novels, she studied the cover. "I'm a sucker for romance, though."

Meagan smiled despite the alarm she felt at Alexis's words. *Books? Dull?*

"What would you suggest?"

Meagan tugged down a contemporary romance and placed it in Alexis's hands. "This one is great. The author writes beautiful stories, and there's an abundance of romance."

"Maybe." Alexis eyed it warily. "Doesn't have a good-looking guy on the cover."

Meagan pulled down another. "How about this? Two people meet on a cruise and sparks fly."

Alexis grinned. "I love a good cruise. I'll take it."

"Very good. Let's go ring it up."

"Cool."

Alexis's phone rang, and she followed Meagan to the register, talking to the caller as she walked. "Yeah?" A pause and sigh. "I already told you. I want my clothes back from the dry cleaner's today. Not tomorrow." More silence. Then Alexis's voice rose. "I don't care what the cleaners say. They should have had it done already. Twenty-four hours is plenty of time to clean and press a few dresses." She slapped the book on the counter. "Just tell them to get a move on." She ended the call with a huff. "Ridiculous."

Meagan swallowed and quietly rang up her purchase. "Problem?"

"It's my new housekeeper." Pulling out her wallet, she yanked a plastic card free. "I don't know why my mother kept her around."

Meagan put on her most innocent smile. "Does your mother no longer employ her?"

Alexis scowled. "My mother recently died and I inherited everything."

Meagan studied the woman. *Is Alexis speaking of the fortune she hopes to receive?*

She prayed her face didn't betray her thoughts as she rang up the sale. "Fifteen dollars and eighty-seven cents."

Alexis handed her the card. As she slid it through the credit card reader, Meagan said softly, "I'm sorry to hear about your mother."

"Me too." The woman tossed her hair back over her shoulder. "No one knows what I've suffered lately. I miss her. I admit we didn't always get along, but no one else had my back the way she did."

"I'm sure that's true. Moms are like that." Piper's meeting with the housekeeper drifted through her mind. Alexis and Honey had quarreled not long before Honey's death. "What did you two argue about?"

"Anything. Everything." She accepted her card back from Meagan. "Mother never approved of my choice in men, my clothes, my interests. You know what mothers are like."

Meagan managed a small smile in return. She missed her parents something fierce. The distance between Nantucket and Arizona seemed to stretch farther apart with every passing week. Based on this conversation, she doubted she'd ever had a disagreement with her mother like Alexis had with hers.

The printer hummed as it produced the sales receipt. Meagan tore it off and handed it to Alexis. "I hope you can find comfort in the coming days. Losing a loved one is difficult."

"Retail therapy helps." Alexis stuffed the receipt in her purse and pulled out sunglasses, sliding them on with a coy smile. "Meeting handsome men doesn't hurt either. In fact, I have a lunch date with one in fifteen minutes."

"Where are you eating?"

"I texted my mother's lawyer—best-looking man I've seen in ages—and we're sharing a meal at the Clam Bucket Café."

She was eating with Luke? Whatever the reason, Meagan was sure Luke had a good one. She fumbled for a reply. "How nice."

"Isn't it?" Snatching up the book, Alexis wiggled her fingers in a farewell gesture. "Thanks for the recommendation."

"Anytime."

She tossed a smile over her shoulder. "Who knows? If this date goes well, I may not need to read a romance book. I might be living one."

Meagan forced another smile. Glancing at the clock on the back wall, she bit her lip. Hattie would arrive soon to take the afternoon shift. Usually, Meagan used Hattie's help on the floor to catch up on the financial end of the business. Not today. Something more pressing had sprung up.

She needed to talk to Luke about her latest visitors.

21

Luke

Luke checked his watch. Alexis had asked him to meet her at the Clam Bucket Café at noon. It was twenty minutes past, and she was still absent.

He figured he might as well eat. Waving over the waitress, he ordered an iced tea and a grilled chicken salad.

As he handed back the menu, Alexis breezed in. Chunky bracelets clinked on her wrists. A breezy hot-pink blouse was adorned with multiple necklaces. Plucking the sunglasses off her nose, she offered him a dazzling smile before sitting down and placing her massive purse on the floor beside her.

Luke lifted a brow, his eyes focusing on a stain on the woman's shirt. "Run into trouble on the way here?"

"What? No. Why?"

"No reason."

She twisted in her seat and frowned. "Where is the waitress? I should have a menu already."

He resisted the urge to roll his eyes. The waitress reappeared with his iced tea. "Thank you."

"No problem." She turned to Alexis and pulled out her notepad. "Something to drink, ma'am?"

A flicker of irritation marred Alexis's brow, but she forced out a clipped smile. "Diet soda and a king club sandwich. And for the record, I'm not a ma'am."

The waitress tossed Luke a glance. "Of course. One diet soda for you, *miss*."

When their server had hustled away, Alexis smiled widely. "Look at us. It's almost like we're on a date."

He couldn't let that idea gain traction. "Except we're not."

She laughed breezily. "You're no fun. You must get your share of dates, what with being a lawyer and so handsome and all."

The woman had been here less than five minutes and her company already exhausted him. "You wanted to talk about your mother, Miss Northcutt?"

"It's Alexis." She dropped the bubbly façade and straightened. "Yes. I still can't believe the results of the autopsy. Isn't it awful?"

"It is," he agreed.

"I suppose that means it won't be long now until her will can come out in the open. I am so sick of this wait-and-see nonsense."

"I'm afraid you still have to wait and see," Luke replied. "The police have started an investigation."

She paled, playing with a ring on one of her fingers. "That's terrible too. So awful."

"I can't help with that, but I do have news about the will." Luke slid an envelope across the table. "Here is a notice that you are indeed a beneficiary."

She snatched the envelope and scanned the note inside. "This is great, but I don't understand. If you know what my mother wanted me to have, you should tell me what it is already and let me move on."

"It's not that easy."

"Why not?"

Taking the lemon from the rim of his glass, he squeezed the juice into his iced tea. "Because when an estate goes to probate, procedures must be followed. It's a process that allows the judge to prove a will is a valid public document."

Alexis's eyes narrowed. "Why would my mother's word not be enough?"

"Everything must go through due process. The court has to make sure your mother's wishes are carried out legally and completely. I can't bend the rules."

"Isn't that convenient?" Acid dripped from her voice as she crossed her arms. "I wouldn't be surprised if you were planning to take some money for yourself. Hiding details and whatnot sounds fishy to me. You don't want any of us to get anything, do you? Maybe Uncle Victor was right."

Suddenly he's Uncle Victor. "Your mother came to me, Alexis. Not the other way around." He took another sip of his tea. "The very fact that the court had me contact you about the hearing proves you're a beneficiary. That means you will get something. What is this really about?"

"What do you mean?" Panic flickered in her eyes.

"I saw you talking with your uncle Victor earlier. You two didn't agree on anything a week ago." He lifted a brow. "And here you are now, getting along."

She swallowed and looked away. "I—we—" Her shoulders slumped. "Fine. I'll tell you. Uncle Victor is worried about what will happen if my brother gets his hands on Mother's money. And I agree with him."

Luke resisted the urge to groan. Was this Victor's attempt to edge into part of the family inheritance—setting siblings against each other? "You don't want him to have a share?"

"It's not that." She dropped her head in her hands, digging her perfectly manicured nails into her hair. "I love Hunter, but he's a train wreck. Always has been. You know what he did the last time Mother gave him money, don't you? His actions tore up this family. I won't have him do that again."

The waitress returned with their plates. "Need anything else?"

"Not at the moment. Thank you." Luke offered her a smile and turned his attention back to Alexis as the waitress bustled away. "People change, you know."

"Sometimes. And admittedly, I haven't been around Hunter much since he was incarcerated. But how do I know he's not going to pull the same stunts all over again?"

"You don't." Picking up his fork, he poked at the salad on his plate. "Legally, though, trying to manipulate the situation could make things worse."

She offered him a curt nod. "I guess that's a risk I'm willing to take."

"Be that as it may, in this situation, I have to follow the letter of the law. My hands are tied."

She rose and snatched the strap of her purse. "Fine. I've heard enough anyway."

"Alexis?"

"What?" she snapped.

"Try giving your brother a chance. You may be surprised. Don't we all deserve a second chance?"

The irritation drained from her face, replaced with a familiar sadness that defined all the Northcutts he had met. But before he could ask about it, she strode out of the café.

Luke shook his head. This whole situation had the potential to rip Honey's family apart for good.

22

Meagan

$\mathcal{M}$eagan sighed, peering out the window at the parking area in front of Luke's law firm. She saw neither his car nor his bicycle there. She supposed she would have to wait until later to tell him her findings about today.

She was too restless for her quiet, peaceful store. She'd swing by the repair shop to see if the coolant had been delivered.

She left the store in Hattie's capable hands and drove the short distance to Al's Auto and Motor. Rolling down her window to enjoy the afternoon breeze, she inhaled the scent of blooming flowers and coming rain. Pewter clouds clogged the sky as thunder grumbled overhead. She couldn't keep the window down for long.

She pulled in as the first drops began to fall. A police cruiser sat outside the building. She rolled up the window and killed the engine. *Why are the police here?*

Entering the shop, she shook off the raindrops that had pelted her clothes and eyed Bryce Hanson, Nantucket's deputy police chief. He was busy talking with the man behind the register. Whatever was going on must be important for him to have come.

The deputy chief held a notepad and was writing down information, his face stern. "You say you noticed fallen shingles all over the steps when you arrived?"

"That's right, sir. I was just getting out of my car when I noticed them. It struck me as weird because last night we didn't have a storm or anything that could push them off the roof like that. And then when I went inside, everything looked a mess. Strangest thing."

Meagan tensed. Had the repair shop been broken into like so many other businesses?

Hanson eyed the corners of the store and gestured with his pencil. "I see you have security cameras installed. Have you checked them yet?"

"Not yet. I thought I should call the police first." He pulled out a small cashbox from underneath the counter. "I always leave this in the back room, in case I have petty cash that needs to be dropped off at the bank the following day." The clerk flipped the lid open. A neat stack of green bills remained inside. "Everything is here. Why would someone break in, make a mess, and then leave without taking anything?"

"Any other employees here last night?"

"No sir." The employee glanced at Meagan. "Be with you in a minute, miss."

"No problem."

"Are you sure nothing is missing?" the deputy chief pressed.

"Not that I've noticed." He shrugged his thick shoulders.

Hanson tucked the notepad away. "I'd like to take a look around, if you don't mind. We'll also need your security camera footage."

"Yes sir." As the policeman moved to the back, the clerk offered Meagan a tired smile. "Sorry for the wait. It's been a rough day."

"I'm sure it has. I came in to grab some coolant. My refrigerator is trying to die."

"Yeah, Eddie mentioned a lady would be here for coolant. I'm sorry. None has come in yet. Our next order should be in tomorrow."

"I see." *Nan's again for breakfast it is.* There was always a positive. "Guess I don't have much choice in the matter," she said. "Thank you for your time."

"My pleasure. Sorry I couldn't help."

She moved to leave but whirled back, struck by a thought. "I had a question. How often do you sell the coolant?"

"Maybe a few times a month. Why do you ask?"

"No reason. Just curious, I suppose."

"Curiosity killed the cat." He waved a hand. "Usually, we keep more stock on the shelf, but a super-friendly older woman came in needing some the other week. Bought my last two. It was my fault for not ordering sooner, but I didn't realize we were totally out."

Her stomach clenched. "This woman. Can you describe her? Maybe I know her and can borrow some from her."

"She smiled a lot and had one of those short hairdos. Told me about her dog who died. Ring any bells?"

Yes. "A little," she said. "Thank you."

He waved a hand in dismissal. "Don't worry. We'll get your fridge fixed and working in no time. Feel free to come back tomorrow and ask for Bill. That's me." He moved the cashbox back under the register.

"All right. I will. Thanks."

Meagan stepped outside and sprinted to her car. The rain was really coming down now. Tucking herself behind the steering wheel, she took a few moments to collect her thoughts, her pulse racing in her ears.

A woman who may have been DeeDee Davis purchased coolant not long before Honey was poisoned by the same.

Jamming her key in the ignition, she jumped when her phone rang. It was Hattie.

She answered immediately. "Hello?"

"Hey, Meagan? We've got a situation over here."

Meagan gripped the phone tighter. "What's wrong?"

"There's a raccoon in your office." Meagan could hear the panic lacing the older woman's voice. "I heard a rustling sound and thought it was Hash Brown. But then I remembered that you said Nell is watching him.

When I followed the sound, this raccoon took off running—straight to your office. I shut the door so it couldn't escape. I suspect it got into the storage space upstairs and wandered down to the shop. Then it got spooked and took refuge in the only dark place it could find. The customers are concerned and more than a little frightened. What do I do?"

The answer came easily to Meagan. "I'll call animal control. Keep the office door shut. I don't want you or anyone else getting bit. I'll be there in a few minutes."

"Okay. Thanks."

After ending the call, she found the number for animal control, told them about the situation, and drove back to Rose Cottage Books. She used the back entrance and gaped at the sight she found. Hattie stood guard before the office door, a chair propped under the door handle for good measure, while several customers peered through the office window, trying to see the animal within.

Hattie's shoulders sagged with relief when she saw Meagan. "Thank goodness. I've been a nervous wreck, wondering if that thing was tearing up your office."

Meagan squeezed the woman's shoulder. "You've done well. Animal control will be here in a few minutes." She glanced around the bookstore. Everything else seemed to be in place. "How much damage did it do?"

"Not much, at least from what I saw."

"I'll go check." Moving past her office, she headed upstairs to the storage space she shared with her landlord and switched on the lights. Their latest book shipments sat in boxes, waiting to be inventoried and shelved. Shredded cardboard littered the floor near the back. She moved closer and eyed the contents of the ruined box. All the books inside were unscathed. Everything else was in order. There had to be something that would give her a clue to the raccoon's appearance.

She took a step toward the stairs and stopped. Two battered shingles were strewn on the floor. She sucked in a breath and glanced up. A small hole stared back at her—one large enough for a curious critter and several shingles to slip through.

Shingles. Like at Al's Auto and Motor.

Goosebumps peppered her skin as she raced back downstairs.

"Hattie, I think I've solved the mystery of the Nantucket robberies."

Meagan watched the animal control officer gently carry the crate holding the captured raccoon from her office. "Don't worry about him, Miss Poe. We will release him into a more suitable habitat."

"Thank you for your help." She smiled at the bearded officer. "He gave us quite a scare, but I don't wish him any harm."

The man nodded. "By the way, you were right. I checked the roof where the soffit meets the roofline. Typical raccoon work."

"I had no idea they could do that much damage."

"They can also get inside buildings through chimneys, roof vents, and large plumbing. Smart animals."

From the cash register, Hattie shivered. "I'll be checking my house twice when I get home from work."

"Do you think raccoons could be responsible for all the supposed robberies lately?" Meagan asked.

"Absolutely," the officer answered. "And our office has noticed an increase in the local raccoon population."

Meagan turned to Hattie, excitement mounting. "That would explain why there was never any cash taken."

"And why there was such a mess left behind in every business," said Hattie.

The officer lifted the cage. "These guys will get in anywhere they think they'll find food and a nice warm home. We'll work with the police to take care of it." Offering a small salute, he smiled at the women. "Thank you for your help, ladies."

"Thank you for coming to our rescue." Meagan watched him leave, furry little bandit in tow. "What do you know, Hattie? You've helped to catch a famous intruder."

"Just an average Tuesday, right? It was the least I could do." Hattie made her way toward the stockroom. "Now to find a broom and clean up the mess."

"I'll help. One mystery solved." Meagan's smiled faded as quickly as it appeared. *But still another to figure out.* As soon as the cleanup was done, she would contact Luke.

23

Luke

Back at home, Luke sank onto the sofa and tucked his hands behind his head. A headache had pounded the base of his skull all afternoon. Was it from the storm that had blown in? Probably not. The throbbing in his head and tightness in his shoulders was more likely from stress and lack of sleep.

Lunch with Alexis had been unpleasant, but still, it had been nice to take a small break from the office this afternoon. He'd needed a change of scenery and a full meal. Unfortunately, it hadn't taken his mind off the problem. Was Officer Taylor having as much trouble as he was, puzzling out the mess of the Northcutt family?

And then there was Stella. The woman had called him again this morning to insist he put a stop to her son-in-law's comedy act, which, according to her, had "gotten completely out of control." He'd called Antonio, and the comic had insisted he was working hard to change his tune. His mother-in-law was just being difficult. But now Stella was hesitant to continue with mediation. Luke was afraid she didn't actually want reconciliation. She wanted her way.

He rubbed his eyes.

He hoped reading would distract him. He reached for the copy of the book club book resting on the coffee table and flipped to chapter 6: *The tables had turned. No longer was I the hunter but the prey.*

Intrigued, he delved into the reading. He had made significant progress when his phone rang. Sighing, he tossed the book to the side and reached for the device. Meagan's name was on the screen. His chest lightened and he smiled.

"Hey, Meagan."

"Luke?" Her voice was barely above a whisper. "I wanted to talk to you in person, but you're not at your office, so this will have to do. I have to tell you something."

Luke shot upright on the couch, alarmed by her tone. "What's wrong?"

"Today is full of surprises. First, my refrigerator breaks. Then DeeDee appears in the bookstore."

"DeeDee Davis?"

"Yes. She was playing with Hash Brown and told me how much it made her miss her own dog, Oreo, who apparently died by ingesting some car chemicals. Then I overheard her talking to Nan, who called her DeeDee, and I went to my office to talk to the repairman—"

"The repairman?"

She began again, slower, more controlled now. When she got to the part about arriving at the repair shop and meeting someone named Bill, Luke stopped her.

"Who's Bill?"

"The clerk at the store. He told me he's out of coolant right now because a woman bought the last of it a while ago. When he described her, it sounded like DeeDee Davis."

"DeeDee again?"

"Yep." Meagan's voice held a hint of satisfaction and a tinge of excitement. "I mean, she obviously knows the stuff can kill dogs."

"Wait, wait." Luke rose and paced the length of the living room. "You're assuming coolant was one of the chemicals that poisoned her dog. What if it wasn't? You're also guessing that the woman Bill described was DeeDee, but you don't know for sure."

She hesitated. "That's a good point."

"Let's say you're right, and she did buy the coolant. How do you know that she didn't simply need it for her car, or an appliance like yours?"

"I don't know." Silence breathed thick for long moments. "Sorry about that. I'm moving some boxes."

"No problem." He listened as she shifted something else and pondered. *Could DeeDee have killed her best friend? There's only one way to be sure.*

Luke found his keys. "You feel like joining me for an interview?"

More silence. Then, "Are you sure your date can spare you?"

He frowned. "Date? What date?"

"Alexis Northcutt was in Rose Cottage Books today too. She told me she had a date with you at the Clam Bucket Café."

Luke laughed. "I assure you, the meeting with Alexis was not a date. The whole thing was a disaster. I was simply letting her know in an official capacity that she is one of Honey's beneficiaries, and all she wanted was to dig for information about Honey's will."

"Oh."

Was that relief he heard? Or was he thinking wishfully?

"Anyway, I'd like to talk to DeeDee again. You want to go with me?"

"Am I allowed?"

"Yes. We're just having a chat."

"Okay then."

He smiled. "Great. I'll pick you up at Rose Cottage Books in five minutes."

Rain battered the windshield of Luke's Mustang. His stomach churned with the revelation of DeeDee's possible purchase. If she had, it could change everything. But surely the grandmotherly woman couldn't have done such a thing.

As they pulled into DeeDee's driveway, Meagan asked, "What are you going to say?"

"I don't know yet." He narrowed his eyes at the picturesque yellow home with white trim. Rain dripped from the eaves and the honeyed glow of light shone through the living room window. "I'll think of something." His gaze rested on hers, catching warmth in her chocolate-brown eyes. "Keep your phone handy. Maybe use the voice recorder too. If anything happens, Officer Taylor will want to know."

Meagan nodded.

They climbed out of the car and dashed to the front porch, where Luke knocked. A wreath bearing the words *April Showers Bring May Flowers* hung at eye level. *But what do May showers bring?* Luke wondered.

The door opened, and DeeDee smiled out at the pair of them, though her eyes clouded with uncertainty. "Hello." She squinted at Luke. "Mr. Harris, it's good to see you again so soon. Back for more cookies?" Her focus shifted to Meagan. "And I met you at the bookstore a little while ago, didn't I?"

"Yes ma'am."

Confusion lingered on DeeDee's face as she ushered them inside, but Luke suspected she was too gracious to ask why they had arrived at her door. "I just got home, but I can get some coffee on lickety-split. This rain could drown a river otter."

"Thank you." Luke eased into a chair, trying to keep his expression neutral. Despite their suspicions, no one could claim DeeDee wasn't an amazing hostess. He glanced at Meagan, who was watching him. *Follow my lead.* He prayed she could read the silent message in his eyes.

She tipped her chin in understanding.

DeeDee scooted into the kitchen, and soon they could hear clinking and rustling as she worked. "It's nice to have company. Since my husband passed, I do all I can to fill my days, but some are easier than others." Her voice grew stronger as she reentered the living room with a tray of cookies. "There now. You can enjoy these while the coffee brews. What can I do for both of you?"

Luke gestured to Meagan. "My friend here is interested in your card club. What's the game called again?"

"Spades," DeeDee answered. "Funny you mention that. I've been trying to recruit new players, but now I'm not sure we'll resume our games—at least not in the near future. It wouldn't feel right without Honey. Sorry, dear."

"I understand," Meagan assured her. "But I'd love to learn to play if it's not too much trouble. I'm always on the hunt for fun things to learn. Who knows? We might even start our own card group at Rose Cottage Books."

"I'd be happy to teach you," DeeDee said. "Of course, it takes a lot of practice to get good at it. Acquiring tricks, learning how to read your opponent, understanding all the rules. Not everyone loves it the way my friends and I do."

"What is a trick?" Meagan asked.

"The cards you collect as a winning hand. If you have the highest card, you get to gather your opponents' cards and keep them."

"So, it's the collective cards from the group?"

"Yes." Bubbling sounds came from the kitchen. DeeDee rose. "The coffee is almost done. Both of you want a cup, right? I don't believe there's anything like it on a rainy day like today."

Is she changing the subject? "Yes, please. Black," Luke said, trying to keep his tone even.

"You got it." Her gaze swung to Meagan. "And you?"

"I'll take a cup. Thank you. Cream, no sugar."

"Coming right up. Maybe sometime I'll try working as a barista. I'm so used to different coffee orders from the card group." She returned to the kitchen.

Luke called out, "How did Honey take her coffee?"

There was a crash in the kitchen.

Luke and Meagan traded glances, then ran toward the noise.

DeeDee was pale, fumbling to clean shards of glass now scattered all over the floor. "I'm such a butterfingers sometimes."

"It happens to all of us." Meagan checked the woman for injuries—there were none—then searched the space for a broom. "Here. Let me help you clean up."

"No no, you're guests in my home. Please don't fuss. I'm fine. Let me get it," she protested.

Ignoring her, Luke yanked a paper towel from the dispenser and gathered the tiny pieces that dusted the countertop. He figured DeeDee must have dropped the cup as she pulled it from the cabinet.

They set the space to rights, yet the older woman still remained ashen and shaky. Her fingers trembled as she took a new cup from the cupboard. She shook her hands and pasted a smile on her face. "Thank you both for your help."

"No problem. I'm glad you're all right." Luke leaned against the countertop.

DeeDee slowly filled the cups with steaming black coffee. "To answer your question, Mr. Harris, Honey preferred her coffee with sugar."

Hadn't Honey told him in his office that she hated coffee with anything else in it?

"Luke," Meagan whispered, pointing.

Luke's focus snapped in the direction she faced. A bottle of coolant sat on the table.

When DeeDee fixed her with a curious stare, Meagan quickly explained, "My refrigerator is broken and the repairman told me coolant might fix it, but his shop didn't have any in stock. I'm surprised to see some here, that's all."

"Feel free to take the rest of it," DeeDee said. "I don't need it anymore. I hope it works for you."

It was time to drop the charade. "We know, DeeDee," Luke said.

"Know what?" DeeDee set the loaded coffee tray on the kitchen table.

He exhaled. "We know you poisoned Honey."

The older woman laid a hand on her chest. "I did nothing of the sort."

Luke's eyes narrowed. *Nothing of the sort?* Not an outright denial. The language bump raised the hairs on the back of his neck.

"Ethylene glycol was found in her blood," Meagan said, hefting the bottle they'd found. "It's also in coolant."

DeeDee blinked rapidly and dropped into the closest chair, her movements stiff. "I had no idea."

"Why did you do it?" Luke eased into the seat across from her.

Her blue eyes filled with tears. "But I *didn't*." She swallowed hard and shook her head.

He rubbed the back of his neck. All the signs of truth were in that statement. Could he have gotten this whole thing wrong? "We both witnessed your reaction when I asked you about Honey's coffee preference."

DeeDee's chin trembled. "That was because of my—" She clamped her mouth shut.

"What?" Luke asked gently.

DeeDee closed her eyes for a moment before lifting her gaze to his. "I haven't told many people this, but I've been diagnosed with Parkinson's." Tears spilled over, running down her weathered cheeks. "The tremors are getting worse. Please, don't tell anyone."

Luke covered her trembling fingers with his own, feeling rotten for accusing her so blatantly. "I'm sorry. But why do you want to keep it secret?"

"When my husband passed, I struggled so much. I had no purpose. No joy." She swiped at her falling tears. "I finally realized I could serve others by taking them meals, babysitting, volunteering at church or at the senior center—you know, whatever I could do to help. It gave me meaning. A ministry." She shuddered. "But with this illness, if I can no longer drive and serve, what good am I?"

Luke released her hands and moved to pat her back, his chest aching at the confession. "You dropped the cup because of the Parkinson's, not because you had something to do with Honey's death."

"Not a thing." She shook her head, eyes gleaming with determination. "I would never kill Honey. She was my best friend."

The woman was telling the truth. He squeezed her shoulder gingerly. "I'm sorry for accusing you. I thought that with the coolant, the ride home, the timing—"

"I understand. You have to consider everyone who saw her that day." She patted his hand where it rested on her shoulder. "I could never do such a thing to Honey." Her expression cleared as if a revelation dawned. "Kevin."

"Kevin?" Meagan asked.

DeeDee stared at both of them. "He was here the day of our card game."

24

Meagan

Electricity pulsed through Meagan's veins as she watched DeeDee's expression shift from fear to shock.

Luke's eyes narrowed. "Kevin was here the day of your card game? The day Honey died? Why?"

"I'd asked him to give me a bid on treating my roof. He's got some newfangled notion about a chemical that protects shingles." DeeDee waved her hand dismissively. "Kevin is always involved in some new business venture. First it was flipping real estate. Then he tried selling home goods through a pyramid scheme. That was a bust. He's been through a dozen careers in three years. Get-rich schemes if you ask me."

"What happened?"

"Apparently he and Honey had an argument that morning," DeeDee said. "It must have been a humdinger because I'd never seen him so angry. He always doted on her. Treated her like a queen."

"Who told you they had an argument?" Luke asked. "Honey or Kevin?"

"Kevin." DeeDee's lips thinned into a hard line. "He traipsed into my house with his muddy boots after he finished measuring the roof. I could tell something was wrong, so I asked him what gave him such a sour disposition. He told me about their argument. I never thought much about it until now, but when he came into the kitchen for a drink, he saw the coolant."

Meagan handed her a glass of water. "Why do you have coolant?"

"I needed the stuff for my car. It was getting too hot, so I had my neighbor check it out, and he told me it was low on coolant." DeeDee took a drink of the water and gave Meagan a small, grateful smile. "Kevin made some offhanded comment about it. Something along the lines of 'Maybe we should put some of that in Honey's coffee to sweeten her up.'"

"Yikes," Meagan said.

"I thought he was trying to be funny, but I still scolded him for saying it. He went on, saying something about her money being able to provide all the medical care I needed. I was shocked that Honey had told him my diagnosis. She and I were the only ones who knew. At least, I thought we were."

Meagan's heart ached for the woman. What she was going through couldn't have been easy.

"I guess he saw how upset I was and backtracked real quick," DeeDee said. "Do you think he had something to do with Honey's death?"

"What do you think, DeeDee?" Luke asked.

The woman studied her hands. "I've always thought Kevin was flaky, but maybe it's something worse than that."

"It's suspicious, that's for sure," Luke said. "The police need to know all this. I'll contact Officer Taylor. Would you be willing to give him a statement?"

DeeDee nodded. "Yes, of course."

"Thank you." Luke rubbed the dark stubble shadowing his jaw. "Something doesn't make sense, though. Honey told me she liked her coffee black. You said she drank it with sugar."

DeeDee laughed, her dismay momentarily pushed aside. "Honey recently tried to take her coffee plain—as part of a healthy-eating kick, she said. But that merely lasted a few weeks, like all her other healthy-living intentions. That woman had a major sweet tooth."

Luke grinned. "I get that. My own father warns everyone of the dangers of sweets as he's digging into a bowl of ice cream."

Meagan pulled the conversation back to the problem at hand. "If DeeDee is correct about all this, what should we do?"

"I was wondering that myself."

The gravelly voice caused Meagan to whirl around. Kevin Chambers's stocky form filled the doorway. Meagan's heart raced as she spied the anger darkening his expression.

Thinking fast, she tucked her phone behind her, out of his view. She ran her fingers over the screen, praying she was tapping the right numbers—911.

Luke moved to shield her and DeeDee, his hands lifted, palms open. "Easy, Kevin."

"What are you doing here, at DeeDee Davis's house?" Meagan asked for the dispatcher's benefit. *If a dispatcher is even listening.*

"I left my tools here when I appraised DeeDee's roof and I need them for another project. Imagine my surprise to discover a cozy little trio dragging my name through the mud." He scowled. "I've been meaning to talk to you, Mr. Harris."

"About what?" Luke asked.

"The grapevine is all abuzz. Apparently you've been contacting family and friends of Honey's to invite them to the hearing regarding her estate." His eyes narrowed. "Yet no one has contacted me."

"That's because there's nothing to tell you, Kevin."

Meagan swallowed.

DeeDee took her hand and squeezed. Somehow the simple gesture made her feel a little better.

"I want what's mine," Kevin snarled.

Luke lifted his hands. "I'm sorry, but her will doesn't mention you."

"Honey was my girlfriend. You don't honestly think she'd leave me out, do you?" His gaze swung to DeeDee. "What about it, DeeDee? She told you everything. This attorney of hers got it wrong, didn't he?"

She shook her head. "I have no idea what you're talking about."

He sneered and stepped closer, fists clenched at his side. "Don't play innocent. She told me."

"Told you what?"

"Told me she left something for me. She must have told you."

"She never said a word," DeeDee insisted.

Meagan slipped her arm around the trembling woman. How long would it take the police to arrive? Could the emergency dispatcher hear what was going on?

"You're lying." His nostrils flared. "Give it to me."

Luke met his stare with a steely expression. "It's too late, Kevin. The will has already been filed with probate. It's over."

"Undo it." Kevin took a step closer, neck mottled red.

"I can't." Luke's focus was trained on Kevin's face. He was planning something. Fear clutched in Meagan's stomach. *Please, Lord, help the police arrive quickly.*

"I'll take you to court. Honey wouldn't leave me out. She wouldn't." Kevin paused. "Or maybe she thought she was so smart. I bet she changed her will right after one of our arguments. She thought to get back at me, didn't she?" He took another step forward. "But I'm not so easily thrown away."

Something hard jammed into Meagan's hip. The table. Her fingers reached for anything she could use to protect herself in case Kevin attacked.

Then she remembered the coffee. She rested her phone on the table and let her fingers graze the handle of the closest cup.

"I know Chambers isn't your real name," Luke said. "It's York. You have a string of aliases. Bad investments gone wrong? Evading debt collectors?"

Kevin blinked rapidly as sweat dripped from his temple. "You don't know anything. Honey said she wouldn't abandon me."

Luke caught Meagan's eye and gave a nearly imperceptible nod.

Meagan tensed.

A sob escaped DeeDee's throat. "Please believe me. I had no idea what was in Honey's will."

"Unfortunately for you, I don't believe you." Kevin lunged toward DeeDee.

Meagan hurled hot coffee into Kevin's face.

He yelled, and Luke tackled him to the ground.

Luke glanced over his shoulder. "Call the police."

"I already did." She held up her phone, relieved that she'd managed to make the call and that it was still connected. She pressed it to her ear, not sure how she would hear the voice on the other end over the pulse pounding in her skull. "Hello?"

"Yes ma'am. I heard the whole thing," the dispatcher said. "The police are on their way."

DeeDee wrapped her in a tight embrace. The poor woman was trembling badly.

Meagan hugged her back. "It's okay. It's over now."

Kevin growled, unable to move with Luke kneeling on his back. "Nothing's over."

"How, Kevin?" DeeDee asked. "How could you kill Honey?"

"She promised." The man's voice broke.

"Promised what?" Luke urged.

"To help me. My businesses all failed. The creditors are threatening me. She promised to help."

DeeDee stamped her foot. "Of course the creditors are upset. I know how much time you spend losing whatever meager earnings you make. Honey told me everything about that. You've maxed out all your credit cards, and you'll never be able to repay your bank loans. And then you expected her to clean it all up?"

For the first time, Meagan saw fear on Kevin's face. "They'll take everything. I'll be ruined. She promised she'd help." He paused, his voice cracking with emotion. "I never meant to kill her. It was an accident."

"How do you 'accidentally' make someone you love ingest coolant?" DeeDee demanded.

Kevin didn't respond.

"Your own poor decisions led to this." Luke's expression was fierce. "And you'll have to deal with the consequences."

Police sirens approached, and the reflection of the blue-and-red flashing lights danced through the windows.

Meagan ran to the front door and wrenched it open, relief coursing through her.

Officer Taylor and Deputy Chief Hanson filed in, their faces solemn. "What's the problem here?" the deputy chief asked.

Meagan pointed toward the kitchen. "A man, Kevin Chambers, came in here and threatened us. We believe he's responsible for Honey Northcutt's death."

He nodded in understanding. "We'll take care of it. But don't go anywhere yet please. We'll need to get your statement."

She watched as they entered the kitchen to arrest the scowling man. The sound of Luke's baritone warmed her. What would have happened if he hadn't been there?

DeeDee appeared and motioned to the overstuffed sofa cushions. "Let's sit down. I still can't believe it." She shook her head. "How could he kill her?"

"I don't know," Meagan said. "The police will figure it out."

"Am I considered a suspect?"

"No. Kevin confessed." Meagan wiggled her phone. "The dispatcher heard everything, and I think the conversation was recorded too."

DeeDee released a sigh. "Thank goodness." She glanced around the room. "You know, Honey always joked that if she ever wanted to leave a fortune, she'd hide it here, so maybe she did leave him something after all."

"Maybe she did."

DeeDee murmured to herself and rose, shuffling through papers on the coffee table. She opened the TV cabinet and peered inside. "Nothing."

Meagan stood and aided her in the search through closets, drawers, and any hidden cubbyholes, but they returned to the living room, hands empty.

"Oh well," DeeDee said. "Joke's on us."

The police wrapped up the arrest and took their statements, then Officer Taylor hauled Kevin to the squad car.

Deputy Chief Hanson approached them. "Stay close to home, please. We may need each of you for more questioning." He said goodbye and went out to help the officer.

Meagan watched them load Kevin into the police cruiser, his hands cuffed behind his back. *What kind of life leads a man to such desperation?* She shivered.

"I don't know what to do. I can't even think straight," DeeDee said.

Meagan patted her back. "I hate the thought of leaving you here alone."

"Don't worry about me. I'll call my card sisters. I'm sure they'll stay with me tonight." She released a melancholy sigh. "Honey always said we were her safe place."

Meagan smiled. "How lovely."

DeeDee's eyes widened. "So *that's* where she hid it." She made a beeline for a basket resting on her fireplace hearth. Magazines, sudoku puzzle books, and a variety of other knick-knacks spilled over its edges.

Yanking out a box of playing cards, she popped open the tab on the end and tugged the deck free. Two scraps of paper fluttered from the inside of the box to the floor.

Meagan grabbed Luke's arm, excitement mounting.

As DeeDee scanned the papers, tears brimmed in her eyes. "They're from Honey. A treasure for sure, but not what you'd expect. Two letters, one telling me and the others in the card group how much she loved us, and one for Kevin, telling him the same." DeeDee sniffed and held the letter to her chest. "Very special indeed."

Meagan knelt at the older woman's side and put an arm around her shoulders. "What a beautiful gift."

"Letters from her heart, so we can keep her with us. Thank you for helping me find them," DeeDee said to Meagan.

"I can't take credit. That was all you."

Luke smiled. "Honey was a smart lady."

DeeDee wiped the tears from her eyes. "Didn't I tell you? Spades is a game of tricks, and Honey played it better than anyone."

25

Luke

"So how did Kevin poison her?"

Luke bit back a smile as Piper propped her chin in her hands on the table at Aunt Maisie's on Wednesday morning, her blue eyes bright.

Meagan chuckled as she stirred her tea. Her laughter lightened his weary mood.

"You won't be happy until you get the lowdown, will you?" Luke asked, feigning exhaustion.

Piper waggled her eyebrows. "Of course not. I am, after all, a journalist. Some would say a sleuth."

"Some might," Luke murmured as he sipped his coffee.

Piper shot him a mock glare. "Some thanks I get for helping you."

Meagan glanced around the restaurant. "Keep it down, please. The place is quiet for a change, and I'm glad, because we aren't supposed to talk about this much. At least, not until the police have officially closed the case."

"That's true," Luke said.

Piper whipped a folded copy of the *Dolphin Gazette* from her bag and set it on the table. "Hate to tell you, but the cat's about to escape the bag. Oh, and check this out." Flipping the newspaper in their direction, she underlined the headline with a nail-polished finger. "Front page and everything."

Meagan read the headline out loud. "'Mysterious Thieves Caught: Raccoons Responsible for Nantucket Break-Ins.' And here's a picture of the animal control officer who came to Rose Cottage Books. That's so nice."

Luke read the article over Meagan's shoulder. "'Thanks to a tip from Meagan Poe, owner of Rose Cottage Books, the mystery surrounding break-ins and vandalism at local businesses on and around Old Wharf Street has been solved. Both the police and animal control confirm that the culprits are none other than the original masked bandits—raccoons.'" Luke nudged her. "Great work."

"When were you going to tell us this?" Piper arched a brow.

Meagan shrugged with a shy smile. "With all the activity at DeeDee's, it slipped my mind."

Luke glanced back down to continue reading. "'An animal control officer captured one of the critters on Tuesday when it found its way into Rose Cottage Books. The officer said the owner discovered shingles inside, near the soffit along the back of the building, and deduced how the raccoon got inside. Police reported similar damage done to Al's Auto and Motor. Video surveillance from the Nantucket store caught a different raccoon gaining access via the same methods on Tuesday morning. The other stores vandalized will also be investigated, but animal control is confident they have found the cause of the break-ins. All raccoons apprehended by animal control will be rehomed to a wildlife refuge.'"

Meagan grinned. "I knew it."

"What?" Piper's brows lifted.

"I was at the repair shop when Deputy Chief Hanson was investigating the break-in." Handing the paper to Luke, she wrapped her hands around the warm cup of tea. "So the video surveillance caught it all. That's a relief."

"Definitely." Luke finished scanning the rest of the page.

"I was starting to think I needed a security system."

"Good news is that you don't," Piper said.

"Yes. It's one less thing to worry Larry about," said Meagan.

Luke handed the paper back to Piper, who said, "Enough stalling. Tell me about all the fun you two had solving crime and whatnot, like a regular Sherlock Holmes and Nancy Drew."

"I wouldn't say it was fun," Meagan replied. "Kevin Chambers, York—whoever he is—was dangerous." She grimaced. "If Luke and I hadn't been there, he might have hurt DeeDee."

"You were smart to call the police right in front of him, but where he couldn't see."

Meagan shot Luke an appreciative smile. "Luke was keeping Kevin's attention on him. The rest was pure luck."

"Think of the next headline," Piper said, her tone almost dreamy. "'Attorney and Bookstore Owner Save Woman's Life When Madman, Teetering on the Edge of Sanity, Bursts into Home.'" Her eyes glowed as the words rolled off her tongue.

Luke took a sip of his coffee. "Sounds awfully long for a headline."

"Well, what would you suggest?"

"'Nosy Reporter Dunks Sleeve in Eggs, Witnesses Say.'"

"Huh?" She looked down. "Very funny."

Meagan giggled and handed her a napkin.

"Okay, but seriously. How did Kevin kill her?" Piper asked.

Meagan adjusted her glasses, expression sobering. "We told you he was working at DeeDee's house that day, correct?"

"Yes."

"Apparently, after he confided in DeeDee about his fight with Honey, he went back out to finish the roof estimate. When he heard the card group arrive, he snuck back into the kitchen and poured coolant into her coffee cup."

"Wait." Piper held up a hand, brows furrowed. "How did he know which cup was hers?"

"Those ladies are at DeeDee's so often that they each have their own designated cup," Luke said. "DeeDee had them made up as gifts, personalized with their names."

Piper shook her head. "I bet she never imagined someone would misuse them that way."

Meagan pushed her plate away. "Kevin claims, if you can believe him, that he meant to put enough in her coffee to make her sick. He wanted to nurse her back to health so she would appreciate him and help him with his debts."

"Not the smartest of plans," Luke said.

"What about the rest of the Northcutt family?" Meagan asked. "They caused you such a headache."

"They are a consequence of broken family ties, greed, and hurt feelings. None of them were involved in Honey's death. Just ready to take her money. They'll figure out their problems somehow, I'm sure."

Piper tapped her finger against her chin. "How do you think Kevin will plead?"

"I have no idea." Luke propped his arms on the table's edge. "All I know is I'm glad I'm not a defense attorney."

In the quiet of his office, Antonio and Stella sat across from Luke, the two of them finally coming to an agreement after nearly an hour of discussion. Luke was happy Stella had heard him out when he'd phoned her yesterday and she'd come on her own terms today.

"Okay," Luke said. "You've both told me you're ready to do things differently. Why don't you talk about that? Mrs. Jones, why don't you start? Do you have anything you'd like to say?"

The woman faced Antonio. "I've thought a lot since our last meeting. And I want to say I've been wrong about so many things. I know we've had some bumps along the way, and with Mr. Harris's help, I've realized my anger comes from hurt." She patted his arm. "You're becoming a successful comedian, Antonio. You've done well for yourself. I admit I'm surprised at that, but also deep down I'm glad. You truly love what you do. However, when people began teasing me about jokes from your show, it was too much for me."

Compassion warmed Antonio's face. "I'm sorry, Stella. I should have thought about how much my act could upset you—or anyone I included in it."

"Thank you. Yes, I was hurt, but I should have come to you directly instead of lashing out in anger and threatening legal action." She shot Luke a smile. "And I'm thankful to you, Mr. Harris, for attempting to calm my temper at every turn in this wild road and not react with haste."

Luke smiled.

She released Antonio's arm. "It's all over and done." Inhaling a deep breath, she swallowed. "If you need to keep telling those jokes, Antonio, I understand."

He shook his head. "No. There's no need."

"What do you mean?"

Antonio relaxed against his chair. "I am writing new comedy material, like Mr. Harris suggested. It's pretty fun—and completely different. I'm focusing most of my content on the fun and joy of children. Great, huh? I tested it out at a few of my shows this week, and I think it gets more laughs than my old stuff. It's still relatable, but not at my family's expense."

Luke's brows lifted. "That's wonderful news. And what about your upcoming television special?"

"We're still in negotiations, with the understanding that kid material will be a big part of the show." He offered Stella a smile. "Better material."

"Oh, thank you!" Stella closed the space between them and drew her son-in-law in for a hug. "I'm so happy."

He released her with a grin. "Missy and I are too. We didn't like having this difficulty hanging over all of us. Especially now. Here." He pulled a small envelope from his pocket and offered it to Stella.

She opened it and read the contents. Her chin trembled as she grinned. "It's a note from Missy. I'm going to be a grandmother."

Antonio scooped her into another hug. "Missy thought this might be a fun way to tell you. We have a note for Roger too."

"It's perfect. Thank you. I know Roger will be thrilled."

"Congratulations." Luke rose and stepped around the desk, offering warm handshakes to the two. "I'm so happy for you both."

Stella's eyes shone. "Goodness, I need to go shopping. You two will need everything—a stroller, diapers, a baby swing, a crib, clothes." She grabbed her purse, slipping her arm through Antonio's. "Do you think Missy is busy right now? We could pick her and Roger up and have a day out as a family."

Antonio squeezed her hand. "As a family," he echoed quietly. As they moved toward the door, Antonio waved over his shoulder. "Thanks again, Mr. Harris. For everything."

Luke nodded as they left. This was why he did what he did. To mend families.

All's well that ends well.

26

Piper waited as the computer's video chat system connected to Cooper's line. She pictured him waiting, hands folded, in his office, which was housed on an upper floor of a modern skyscraper in the heart of Boston. She smiled, remembering the hum and noise of activity that buzzed around her on visits to the place. *Sounds of a business at work.* Today they'd decided to chat virtually, to save her a trip to the mainland. She was glad for that. There was nothing she enjoyed more than the freedom to work remotely and spend time in her home office with Ulysses tucked under her desk, warming her feet.

Finally, the call connected, and Cooper waved at her, the chat screen reflected in his glasses. He wore a button-down with patches on the elbows, a style he favored in warmer weather, when his habitual suede jacket and vest would have been sweltering. "Piper," he said, his neatly trimmed mustache moving as he talked. "So nice to see you again. Thank you for taking time to talk. Are you well?"

"Fine, thanks. You know me. I'm always up for a chat on a Thursday. What can I do for you?"

"I wanted to touch base, really. Your secret-shopper article was a hit. I could tell you enjoyed writing it—despite the one mishap."

Piper shuddered, remembering the time she'd had. The lip-plumping gloss had been a mess. Jim had given her anti-inflammatory medication, but it had still taken a couple of days for her lips to feel normal again. For once, she'd been grateful she didn't have to do in-person interviews for her work. She was sure she would have scared off even the hardiest interviewee. Poor Jim and Ulysses had been scarred enough, and they were her family. "It's why you pay me the big bucks."

Cooper chuckled. "That got me thinking. I would like to add more investigative beauty articles to the column every now and then—celebrity scoops, hard beauty truths, and seasonal pieces. With your knowledge and background in investigative journalism, I wondered if you'd be interested in that."

Piper grinned. "That would be excellent."

"Fantastic. Your first assignment could be a piece on all the blunders in buying beauty products."

"Sounds right up my alley. I'll call it 'Buyer Beware.'"

Cooper grinned. "That's the spirit. The fact is, you're doing an excellent job, Piper. The company continues to receive wonderful feedback on your work."

She was touched. "Thanks."

"You still miss writing hard-hitting journalism?" Cooper asked gently.

"At times. Old habits die hard. But I'm finding new ways to scratch that itch." Helping Luke had satisfied a need she hadn't sensed in a while.

"I'm glad to hear it. I'll keep doing what I can to help you there, but never underestimate the power of the written word, even when it's beauty rather than the bigger stories. What if someone reads about your reaction to the lip gloss and decides to research the ingredients before they buy it, then discovers that it contains something they're deathly allergic to? Then you've saved someone's life."

"I never thought of that." Piper recalled a friend of hers who for years had written light, funny stories for a publisher instead of the deep, soul-stirring anguish she had always envisioned. Her friend had belittled her own abilities until a sweet card from a reader changed her perspective. The woman was a cancer patient and told her friend that the comical stories cheered her up on her toughest days. Yes, journalism was a beautiful profession, even if her career path looked much different than she had envisioned.

"I think you're right, Cooper. The small things really are the big things, aren't they?"

"Absolutely."

Lip gloss reactions and all.

27

Meagan

Saturday meant the return of book club—and the return of Meagan's famous lemon cake. The way her friends raved about it, Meagan was beginning to wonder how much of book club was about the books and friendship, and how much was about the dessert.

Meagan carried the lemon cake to the table, Olivia on her heels with a tray of fruit. Meagan was happy that her refrigerator at home had been fixed and was once again reliably storing food and book club snacks.

"So, she was poisoned?" Olivia's voice rang with disbelief. Honey Northcutt's murder had eaten up the town once the investigation concluded, Olivia among them.

Meagan deposited the cake on the table and bent over to scratch Hash Brown's head. "Yes. Her boyfriend did it by accident. It's all very sad." She went to grab a plate of chocolates to add to the growing spread of food on the table. The bonbons were a thank-you gift from DeeDee. Snagging one, she bit into the creamy texture. It was like silk. Green smoothies in the morning meant comfort chocolate in the evenings—and oh, did she need some comfort with all the drama in her life lately.

Olivia grabbed a coffee cup and filled it, stirring in equal parts cream and sugar. "It sounds like you, Luke, and Piper did a great job working together. How many lawyers can file a client's will *and* solve a murder? If I ever need legal help, I'm calling him for sure."

"He's good at what he does." Warmth crept up Meagan's neck. Actually, Luke was good at a lot of things. She glanced at her copy of the book club book resting on the table. "Were you able to read much of our book this week?"

"I finished it in a couple of days. I couldn't put it down." Olivia set down her coffee and headed to the front of the shop. "I almost forgot. I brought peanut caramel brownies for sustenance. They're still in the car."

"Need any help?"

Olivia waved away the question. "No, I'm good. Back in a sec."

Meagan grinned. "When the others arrive, we'll get started." Mimicking a villainous laugh, she added, "But be ready. I think this discussion might see more literary sparring."

Olivia laughed and ducked out the door.

Meagan eased into the closest chair and smiled when Hash Brown trotted over, his ears perked and his head tilted. She patted her lap and he jumped up, snuggling close. "Maybe I should have chosen something to read other than a mystery, Hash Brown. We've already lived through enough of that these past few weeks."

The little dog wagged his nub of a tail and yipped before licking her chin.

Meagan patted his head. "But remember that our friends wanted a mystery too. I can tell you're as excited to see them as I am." Warmth seeped through her. "And you should be. Friends are so important in life. We're very lucky to have great ones here with us every week—for book talks, adventures, advice, and a little bit of suspense."